"Use your head, princess,"
Kirk growled. "Grizzlies and
hypothermia aren't the only
dangers up here."

With a sudden tug, he jerked her toward him. She
fell against his body, helplessly snarled in her
nightie and the powerful arms he wrapped around
her. His soft lips moved toward her ear, making her
pulse beat faster.

"How innocent are you, Darryn?" he whispered
hoarsely. "Do you need me to show you all
the dangers?"

Other writers have often told me that books are the children you conceive on your own, without help from your husband. Yet every time I finish a book, I find bits and pieces of my husband all through the hero. Here I thought I could create the perfect male all by myself, yet when it comes down to it, I must still think (even after diapers and adolescents and midlife crises) that the perfect male is my husband, Fred Donich. This book is dedicated to him with my love, and to all his belayers who have brought him safely home to me from the mountains, especially:

Our beloved friend,
Tony Rich

Tony died in a massive rockfall on September 25, 1994, while climbing the north face of Granite Peak. Tony's courage and joy in living touched everyone he knew, and he left behind a vast group of family and friends who loved him dearly. Though he will live always in our memories, all our lives are diminished by his death.

Look out in December for Catherine Leigh's next book, *One Night Before Christmas*: *Carly Underbrook loves the holiday season, but to her it's always been more about giving than receiving. Only this year, after a whirlwind romance with cynical tycoon, Jonah St John, Carly learns that Santa's bringing her a little something extra for Christmas…Jonah's baby!*

Beyond Riches
Catherine Leigh

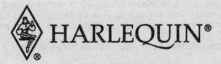

HARLEQUIN®

TORONTO • NEW YORK • LONDON
AMSTERDAM • PARIS • SYDNEY • HAMBURG
STOCKHOLM • ATHENS • TOKYO • MILAN • MADRID
PRAGUE • WARSAW • BUDAPEST • AUCKLAND

ISBN 0-373-17379-2

BEYOND RICHES

First North American Publication 1998.

CHAPTER ONE

WHAT on earth had Darryn Langtry gotten herself into? With trepidation, she watched the four-wheel-drive van, the last attachment it seemed to civilization, disappear into the distance. She turned to the three men who'd ridden out here—wherever here was—with her from the Billings, Montana, airport. They seemed unalarmed by the isolation of this mountain meadow surrounded by obviously impenetrable forest, where the driver had told them to wait for their guide, Kirk Storm.

"Don't look so worried." The one named Alex patted Darryn's shoulder. "You've done this before."

Darryn gave him a weak smile and nodded vaguely. Actually, *they'd* done it before. She'd never been back-packing in her life.

Despite the fact that they'd had to fly to Billings from all over the country, and she'd lived there all her life, these men had more experience in her native state than she did. At least in this wild part of it.

Darryn worried her bottom lip with her teeth. She'd had to tell a small...um, exaggeration about her wil-derness experience to get on this trip. As she looked around, she wondered what had possessed her.

If she weren't so uncomfortable from all that coffee she'd drunk, she might be stewing up a big snit at her half brother, Jordan West, who had recommended Storm Expeditions so highly for her backpacking education. But that seemed beside the point right now.

One of the men motioned at a tiny figure emerging over the horizon. "Must be Kirk."

Kirk Storm approached them with a speed that sur-prised her. From all Jordan had told her about this guy, she expected him to be ten feet tall with a body resembling an Olympic weight lifter at peak steroidism. But Kirk couldn't be an inch over six feet, and though obviously muscular, he looked lean rather than bulky. He'd let his unruly blond hair, which needed a comb, grow long enough in back that it curled over the collar of his khaki shirt.

And though he'd undoubtedly seen a razor more recently than a barber, Darryn couldn't call him clean shaven. What must be at least a two day growth of blond whiskers outlined his square jaw and nearly hid the cleft in his chin.

Of course, as the agent had mentioned to her, Kirk remained in the wilderness for most of the summer. He probably hadn't bothered much about haircuts and shaves. And she had to admit that the golden color of his hair was exactly the shade she'd tried to achieve last time she'd frosted hers.

Pursing her lips as she studied him, Darryn's regard suddenly reached the man's silvery eyes and her thoughts stopped. She couldn't remember ever seeing a look of greater distaste on anyone's face. Darryn felt like something loathsome he'd found on the sole of his shoe.

"Kirk," one of the men said, sticking out a hand. "Will Johnson, remember me?"

Kirk gave him a brief smile while they shook hands, but his gaze immediately returned to Darryn. "Who the hell are you?"

"Darryn Langtry," she said, wishing she felt enough confidence in this alien place to put more haughtiness into her voice. "Surely you know who signed up for your trip?"

"Darryn?" Kirk asked, his tone expressing shock. "Darren is a man's name."

"Not the way I spell it," Darryn assured him.

Kirk's frown deepened. " 'Darryn'," he muttered. "It looked like a typo."

"I didn't name myself," Darryn said acidly. "My father did. He thinks it sounds like, darling."

"Great," Kirk groaned. "Daddy's darling, just what we need." He gestured at the others. "Only men signed up for this trip."

Darryn straightened her shoulders. "I can assure you, Mr. Storm, that's not true. Believe me, I'm not a man and I did sign up for this trip." She glanced around. "Or do you have some conveyance in your pocket that can carry me back to Billings?"

"No such luck—for either of us." He glared in the direction the van had disappeared. "That van won't be back for three weeks. I'm...*we're* stuck."

Uttering a sibilant oath, Kirk turned away disgustedly. For what seemed an eternity, he stared at the mountains in the distance. Darryn glared at him, just as angrily. Probably with a great deal more anxiety.

Her eyes traced his form. He really did have a nearly perfect body. Of course, with all the outdoor exercise he got, he wasn't likely to get rolls of fat hanging over the waistband of his jeans. Nor, her eyes continued lower, a lot of sagging denim over those very masculine hips and buttocks. Nor...

The jeans turned and Darryn found herself staring at his fly. Nothing out of shape there either, she thought as heat stole into her cheeks. Now what? Did she continue to stare at his most personal parts or raise her gaze to those stormy eyes, no doubt angrier than ever catching her ogling him. Or perhaps she should conduct this conversation staring at her feet? That would hardly make him take her very seriously.

"Miss Langtry?"

She looked up, surprised to find humor flashing in the warm gray eyes that met hers. "Yes?"

"It is 'miss', isn't it?" he asked.

Darryn stiffened. "Do you know the marital status of these men?" she asked, gesturing at her fellow campers.

"No, of course not," Kirk said. "I just—"

"Then you needn't know mine!"

Kirk released a long-suffering sigh. "I just wondered," he bit out, "if you brought a husband or your Daddy darling to share a tent with?"

"Oh." Darryn deflated. "No. I came alone."

Kirk nodded slowly, letting his gaze slide over her the way she had studied him earlier. Darryn refused to squirm but she had never wished harder for extra height. How she'd love to look down on this overbearing man, or at least return his gaze from near his level. At five feet one in bare feet, Darryn didn't remember ever enjoying that particular equality with a man.

"We sleep in two...'man' tents," he said. "You'll have to share mine."

"Don't kid yourself, Mr. Storm," Darryn said. "I'll share no one's."

"You think I bring an extra tent just for the pleasure of adding weight to my pack?" he shrugged. "You can share my tent or sleep alone in your bivi sac."

"Bivi sac?" Darryn asked.

Kirk's eyes narrowed at her. "You damn well better have a bivi sac," he growled. "Did you bring everything on the list I sent?"

"Of course," Darryn snapped. "I am perfectly capable of following a shopping list. Besides I had help."

"No doubt daddy took you to all the best stores."

"Actually, he couldn't take time from his practice. He's a highly respected cardiac surgeon and rarely gets days off." The lift of Kirk's right brow made Darryn uncomfortable. She did tend to run on about Daddy. "But my brother went with me. So if bivi sac was on your list, it's in my pack. With my zero bag."

She'd spent days wondering what Storm Expeditions meant by "zero bag". Until Jordan took her shopping and explained that it meant a sleeping bag designed to keep her warm at zero degrees.

"Zero degrees!" Darryn had felt better when she'd thought it a bag for carrying zeros. She had no desire to go camping at zero degrees. What did—?

"Take it easy, Dar." Jordan patted her arm. "You won't be out at zero degrees. The bag is just a precaution. Here give *me* the equipment list. You go get the clothes."

"But just because I have a bivi sac," Darryn told Kirk witheringly, "doesn't mean I plan to sleep in it outside a tent." She tossed her head, remembering belatedly that she'd chopped her long frosted hair to this cap of short black curls to make shampooing easier on this expedition. Unfortunately it also made head-tossing pretty ineffective.

Kirk shrugged. "Fine with me, 'darling'," he said. "Love to have the company. Just be glad I'm not putting you in a tent with Yogurt."

Darryn's head began to spin. "Yogurt?"

Darryn was relieved to hear one of the other men laugh. She'd forgotten they were there while she argued with this autocratic guide. But their presence eased the tension that was building to uncomfortable levels.

"Yogurt Vashique is his partner," Alex explained. "He's not so bad. But Kirk's right, you don't want to share a tent with him."

"Let's get going," Kirk said, his tone businesslike. "Your packs are all loaded properly?"

When the others nodded, Darryn did too. She assumed her pack was correctly done, because Jordan had helped her pack it. Despite her opposition, he'd even insisted she leave behind her pencils and sketch pad. Thus at the moment, as Storm Expeditions had instructed, it contained only her clothes, her zero bag (and bivi sac, she supposed), and a few toiletries. Of course, what Storm Expeditions meant by a few toiletries probably didn't exactly coincide with what Darryn meant.

Nevertheless, she thought hoisting the bag, there was plenty more room in this huge device for whatever else Kirk meant to stuff inside.

"The food and equipment's about two miles from here," Kirk explained, "with the rest of our group. This gives you a chance to get used to your packs while they're still fairly light.''

''Two miles?'' Darryn said weakly. ''But I . . .''

''Let's go,'' said Kirk.

Anxiety tightened her stomach as Darryn stared across the huge meadow, hoping that this two mile hike would lead them closer to some sheltering timber. It had never occurred to her that no other women would join the trip to share the female perspective on the inconveniences of camping.

''Let's go, Ms. Langtry.'' Kirk stood waiting, hands on his hips. ''We stay together on this trip.''

Darryn groaned. The other men looked a football field away already. She tightened the chest straps on her pack as Jordan had showed her and started after them with Kirk at her heels. Hearing his light footsteps and even breathing so close behind her made her nearly jog to keep ahead of him.

Her pack wobbled from side to side, and one chest strap rubbed uncomfortably against her right breast with every other step. Obviously she'd settled it wrong, but she didn't have time to stop and fix it now.

Suddenly Kirk stepped in front of her, halting her progress. ''Darryn, you're walking through some of the most beautiful country on earth. Look up at it once in a while. You can study your feet when you get home.''

Shocked to see a broad smile inside that blond stubble, Darryn couldn't help smiling back at him. She'd never seen a face so transformed by a smile—gone was the Satanic look his bushy brows and unruly hair gave him. Instead as the suntan lines around his eyes crinkled and his expression lit with a kind of little boy excitement, she detected at last a very handsome man hidden behind his stern manner. Then she realized, from the direction of his gaze, that his smile was for the scenery around them, not for her.

''Good advice,'' she muttered, hiding her breathlessness by speaking shortly.

Kirk reached toward her breasts. Before Darryn could react, he loosened one strap and tightened another. "Try that." He gestured for her to follow the others.

Darryn took a few steps and found her pack far less wobbly. "Good," she said.

"Then get going and look up."

She did as he told her and found the view breathtaking. The mountain meadow they traversed looked like a huge plateau of gently waving thigh high grasses with a scattering of purple and blue wildflowers. Stands of aspen trees grew in small clusters across the meadow and seemed to crawl up the pine covered hillside, making a light green trail through the dark evergreens.

"I bet it's really beautiful up here in the spring," she said.

"Yeah," Kirk agreed. "It's a field of color then. Wildflowers everywhere. But I like fall too, when nature tones down the brightness." He waved toward the aspens turning golden in the distance.

Darryn nodded, feeling a powerful longing to be in just such a stand of trees stretched out in a lawn chair with a glass of iced tea and a good book.

"But you're not looking high enough," Kirk said. "It's the mountains that are worth looking at. I can beat a wildflower every time, no contest. The mountains...you never know who'll win. No matter how many times you do battle with them, no matter how good you get, they can still beat you."

Darryn had turned to watch his face during this speech, surprised at the depth of emotion such a man would reveal to a near stranger. His eyes glowed when he gazed upwards at the massive range of Beartooth Mountains towering above the treeline.

Darryn looked up at it, too. Then wished she hadn't.

She'd always found mountains an awesome sight—a sight one enjoyed out the window of one's living room or summer cabin.

Looking at the vast wall of jagged snow-topped rock
that extended across her entire field of vision, blocking
two-thirds of the sky and all of the horizon, Darryn
realized "awesome" didn't begin to describe these
mountains: looming, forbidding, threatening, uncon-
querable came closer; but not much.

She was about to enter a wilderness dominated by
those peaks, aided only by a man who did not claim to
have mastered them. Suddenly Darryn knew what on
earth she'd gotten herself into: trouble.

Big, big, trouble.

CHAPTER TWO

DARRYN stared at the pile of equipment, shifted her gaze to the pile of food, then glanced warily around at the men. Everyone had his pack off in front of him, including Darryn, while Kirk gave them the reassuring news that each day their loads would lighten as they ate.

No one looked a bit confident, no matter what Kirk said, that all that stuff would fit in ten packs. In fact, several less than polite comments to that effect had left Darryn's ears burning.

Kirk ended his review of wilderness navigation. "We could all use a break before..." He shot a glance at Darryn, correctly interpreting her silent plea. "Um, I guess we'd better break in shifts," he amended. "Everyone remember hypothermia? Yogurt'll remind you."

As Yogurt, a handsome Frenchman in his late forties, with sexy dark eyes and peppery looking gray black hair, began speaking, Kirk put a warm hand on Darryn's shoulder and nodded her away from the group. Darryn followed gladly.

She'd listened to Kirk talk about balancing the weight, she'd heard his lecture about giardiasis, she already *knew* about hypothermia. After all, Daddy was a doctor, wasn't he?

That's how she'd gotten into this mess in the first place: a doctor. Peter Tretherwell, to be exact, a handsome new cardiologist, trained at Harvard, raised on Maryland's Eastern shore, who was to join Daddy's practice in a few weeks time.

At the cocktail party to introduce him to the Billings medical community, Peter had ignored his prospective partners and focused all his sophisticated charm on

13

Darryn. Whether from the effects of champagne, or Peter's urbane good looks and allure, or her father's request that she make the new doctor feel welcome, halfway through the party Darryn was appalled to hear herself agreeing to take Peter backpacking and show him the mountains.

She should have introduced him to Jordan. But Peter hadn't wanted to see the mountains with Jordan, and at that moment Darryn hadn't really wanted to share Peter with anyone. Besides, she'd reasoned in her overconfident champagne haze, she had a month before Peter actually moved to Billings. That gave her plenty of time to learn about backpacking and mountains before he arrived. Didn't it?

As she flicked her gaze at the Beartooths, then again at the pile of things she would carry into them, she knew she'd already learned as much about backpacking as she ever wanted to know.

"Come on, Darryn," Kirk said, turning away. "So you'll be back in time to load your pack."

Darryn trotted to catch up with Kirk. "Where are we going?"

"*You're* going just over that hill." Kirk pointed ahead.

Darryn blushed furiously and stared at the earth.

Kirk touched a finger beneath her chin and lifted her gaze. Darryn thought she caught a flash of compassion in his eyes over her embarrassment.

He gestured to the hill's crest not far away where Darryn could just see the tops of some scrubby bushes sticking up. "That's it," Kirk said, keeping his tone carefully neutral. "That's as far away as you get on this trip."

Darryn bit her lip. She glanced back at the group. "That's not very far."

"That's my point," Kirk said. "You'll just have to forget privacy for the next three weeks, Darryn. No one goes anywhere alone on these trips. Wandering off alone in the mountains is dumb."

Darryn opened her mouth to tell him what she thought of his high-handed attitude, then shut it again because she didn't want to shout at his back. Good heavens, the man moved fast. Besides, as she started down the hill, she was surprised how abruptly the land dropped away beneath her feet. After only a few steps, she looked back up and found the crest already out of sight.

These hills looked gentle and rolling only when compared to the rocky crags above them. In fact, they were mountains themselves. Darryn raised her eyes to the circle of sky above her, enclosed by peak after stony peak. The sight, and the thought that she was looking at the only roof she'd see for nearly a month, made her dizzy.

When she rejoined the group, Darryn saw that the two large piles had been divided into ten smaller ones. Her red pack leaned against one of them.

"That's your share, Darryn," Kirk said, aiming his thumb at her pack. "I drew for you."

"You're kidding." Her eyes rounded in horror at the stack of food and equipment these men expected her to carry on her back. "It won't fit!"

"Damn right!" grumbled one of the men, kicking at his share.

"I swear, Kirk," Alex said sourly. "You bring more sh—" he glanced at Darryn "...stuff every year."

"It just feels like it the first day." Kirk actually sounded sympathetic.

Alex was unappeased. "Don't give me that. No way will it fit in—"

"You know damn well Kirk can get it in there," Will said grimly.

Kirk looked up from his pack. "You'll be happier if you do it yourself."

"Why?" Darryn asked.

"Because you'll know where everything is," Kirk said, "and we won't have to unpack the whole thing every time we need the peanut butter."

Darryn lifted the quart jar from the top of her pile. It seemed to weigh a ton. "What about freeze dried?"

Kirk rolled his eyes at the heavens. "Someone asks that every trip."

The man named Roger chuckled . . . sort of. "I ask it every year, Darryn. By the third or fourth day, when we've eaten the load down some, I'm glad we're eating real food. You'll be glad too."

If I live three or four days, Darryn thought, picking up a jar of grape jelly.

"We draw these loads a piece at a time, little one," Yogurt said.

It was the first time Yogurt had spoken directly to her since Kirk'd introduced them. She'd wondered if he was shy with women, if that's why he spent so much time in the wilderness. But when his smiling black eyes met hers, she saw at once she'd misread them. Shyness, ha! His eyes danced with enough charm to put her on her guard.

"Kirk drew for you with much care," Yogurt continued. "When all was divided, every man traded something heavy of yours for something lighter of his."

"*Every* man?" Darryn eyed him skeptically. "Even Kirk?"

"In your dreams," Kirk growled.

Yogurt lowered his voice as if he were saying something intimate. "Kirk's load is already a . . . *soupçon*," he held his thumb and forefinger an inch apart, "heavier than the rest."

Darryn returned Yogurt's smile. "Well, I'm glad he didn't thwart your lovely idea. Thanks, Yogurt."

Kirk stepped between them, looking stern. "Quit whining and pack, Darryn."

Darryn studied the men and noticed that they took their clothes out of their packs to put heavier things on the bottom. But she didn't want to pull out her female underthings in front of this male crowd, so she decided to stuff her pile in on top.

Carefully she tested everything in front of her and found the pink and yellow rope the heaviest. In it went. Then the peanut butter and two jars of jelly. Surreptitiously she grabbed the loop at the top of her pack to test its weight. It already felt too heavy to lift.

She wondered what light things the men had given her and what on earth they'd taken from her pile. With a sigh, she threw in several packages of chicken noodle soup someone had taken out of the boxes and restowed in small plastic bags.

"No, Darryn," Kirk said beside her.

"No?" she asked. "You mean, you'll take the soup? How sweet of you. Why not the jelly?"

He chuckled. It wasn't much of one, but it was definitely a sound of humor, directed at her not some mountain peak. "I mean," he told her, "don't put that light stuff in before the stove."

"Stove?" she exclaimed. "Dear Lord, you want me to carry a stove?"

From her pile Kirk picked up a tiny metal and plastic device Darryn would never have recognized as something to cook on. With a mocking look, he placed it in her hands, carefully wrapping her fingers around it.

"Think you can manage that?"

For just a moment, as Kirk's fingers surrounded hers, sandwiching her hands between the cold metal and his warm calloused palms, she felt oddly, but overwhelmingly, comforted by his strength. As if maybe this trip wouldn't turn out to be such a disaster after all.

"It feels lighter than the soup," she said.

Then Kirk withdrew his support. "It won't for long," he assured her with ominous conviction. "And if your pack's too light, I'll trade you the stove for the fuel."

"No thanks." She replaced the soup packages with the stove. "I'm not that stupid."

"I don't think you're stupid, Darryn," Kirk told her back. "Just inexperienced. By the end of the day, I'll know how inexperienced. Then I'll know whether to fire that woman who books my trips.''

Darryn studied her boot tips. ''I wouldn't do that.'' She blushed and turned to her pack.

Kirk didn't answer but he didn't move away either, and she thought she could feel his eyes boring into her. ''Okay,'' he finally said. ''Everyone loaded?''

Darryn tried to lift her pack and a grunt whooshed out of her.

''Not like that, Darryn,'' Alex said, striding over to help her. ''Put your foot up on a rock and lift the pack onto your knee.''

''Oh, right,'' Darryn said. ''How silly of me to forget.''

Lifting the pack the way Alex showed her made it barely possible to get it onto her back, but she didn't believe she'd ever be able to move. When she took her foot off the boulder, she nearly tipped over backwards. Will and Alex caught her and pushed her upright.

Yogurt joined them and helped her tighten her straps. ''You must situate the pack properly between...'' he eyed her lower body with appreciation ''...your hips and shoulders, little one.''

''If one of you samaritans wants to carry Darryn's pack for her,'' Kirk said acidly, ''get it on and let's move out.''

Darryn's three helpers glared at Kirk.

''Any takers?''

Silence greeted his question. ''I thought so.'' He turned to the trail.

Darryn leaned forward and managed to take a step without falling. If she kept the weight exactly balanced between smashing onto her face and tumbling over backwards, she could walk. In fact, with the pack adding all its weight to her forward momentum, she couldn't stop walking. Although, since the pack tugged her from side to side at every step, ''walk'' didn't exactly describe her gait. Stagger was what she'd call it. And, at the pace

Kirk was setting, who knew how long she could keep it up?

As he strode down the trail, Yogurt joined them. "I think she has maladjusted her frame," he said loud enough for Darryn to hear.

"She hasn't," Kirk returned. "I checked. She may have brought too big a pack. I'll see tonight and trade packs with her. If I have to. You know that kind of pack doesn't fit me."

"By tonight, my friend, she will—"

"This trip is only for experienced backpackers," Kirk said. "She shouldn't have brought an untested pack. It'd take an hour to switch them now. And she really won't know till she's hiked with it." He flicked a glance over his shoulder and pack at Darryn. "She knew what to expect when she signed up."

"Very true," Yogurt agreed. "So if she has made the mistake, we shall leave her by the trailside for scavengers to pick over. Then ourselves, we shall not be burdened with her innocence on—"

Kirk glared him into silence. "Do you remember now why I don't take women on these trips?"

"Ah yes, *mon vieux*, I remember very well." Yogurt laughed, sounding terribly French. "And it has nothing to do with inexperience of the trail. As you know, it—"

"You must want to lead, Yogurt." Kirk whirled toward the back of the group. "Go ahead. I'll take the rear."

Yogurt touched the brim of his Colorado Rockies cap in mock salute as Kirk stalked off. If Darryn had had the strength to speak, she'd have thanked Kirk for leaving, because Yogurt set a much slower pace.

But speech was out of the question. So was ever looking up to enjoy the view. It took all her concentration simply to lift her booted feet, one after the other, high enough to step over the roots and rocks that appeared across her path.

She knew they'd entered timber only because the trail grew darker and the pine smell sharper. She knew they were climbing because the trail grew so steep it began to switch back and forth across the mountainside, and occasional patches of snow appeared beneath the brush at the edge of her vision.

Dimly Darryn heard the voices of the men exclaiming over the beauty of a view or their enjoyment of the isolation, or cursing over their pain at such exertion after a year behind desks in three piece suits. Mostly, however, she heard the pounding of her heart, the rushing of blood in her ears, the rasping of her breath wheezing in and out of her lungs.

Days later, or perhaps hours, or maybe only—oh who cared!—Kirk called to Yogurt that it was time to make camp. Darryn almost cried with relief. She stood up straight to rub her back and fell over backwards onto her pack. She didn't care. Without bothering to get up, she undid the chest and hip straps and pulled her arms free.

Then she just lay there, gasping for air, wondering if she would ever breathe normally again. She heard the others setting up camp around her, but she didn't stir. Occasionally someone called her name, laughingly asking if she'd enjoyed the hike. She answered with a grunt.

Now and then, to make sure she hadn't died, she opened her eyes to see if night had fallen. It hadn't. Somewhere far above the evergreen branches overhead was blue sky, not black. The aspen and brush visible from the corner of her eyes hadn't turned brown and lost their leaves, so winter hadn't snuck up on her while she wasn't looking. She closed her eyes again.

"Darryn." It was a command, not a question. So it must be Kirk.

"Everyone's hungry."

"Not me." Darryn was surprised her lips worked so well. It was her lungs that were behaving wrong—her voice came out hoarse. "Maybe water."

"We need the stove, Darryn." Kirk sounded more long-suffering by the moment. "And we need the weight of your pack." His tone turned less demanding. "You've got to eat."

"Not me." She didn't move, didn't open her eyes.

Suddenly her pack rolled, tipping her sideways onto the ground. With a sigh, Darryn curled into a ball.

"Do you want me to dig in here for the stove or do you want to get it out?"

Darryn blinked. On second thought, maybe he really was being patient. After all, she seemed to have the only cooking device for ten people. She found his gaze. "Dig?"

"In your pack." Kirk no longer looked disgusted or impatient. He looked worried. "You've got to eat, Darryn. I'll get you an energy bar."

"Energy," she murmured. "Just what I need."

Darryn listened to Kirk rustling through her pack, strangely unmoved by having someone paw through her personal things. When he found the stove, he walked away. She rolled over to put her weight against the pack again and discovered he'd taken it.

With a groan, she pushed herself to a sitting position. Not far away, on what looked like a bed of rocks at the foot of a snowfield in the shadow of a sheer rock face, five tents stood, their nylon covers flapping in the wind. Against the backdrop of the granite cliff rising behind them, they looked like little yellow and blue mushrooms—as puny and out of place as Darryn felt.

And smaller she believed than any sane person would mean by "two man". She doubted she could make do in that minute space all alone. The thin material didn't look strong enough to offer protection from the elements, much less from wildlife.

And they looked so far away across all those rocks that had obviously fallen off the mountain, crushing each other over the years nearly to gravel. A veritable ocean of rocks, much too unstable to walk on the way she felt now. She put a hand behind her to lie down again. Maybe she'd stay right here on this nice hard dirt of the trail. Except her head was throbbing unmercifully and she'd really like one of the aspirin buried in her pack.

She looked up to see Kirk tossing her pack into the nearest tent. Nearest, but not near enough. The thought of getting to her feet and walking up that scree field made her woozy. She pushed her fist against her mouth as a wave of nausea hit her.

Suddenly a gust of wind caught the tent Will and Alex would share, turned it upside down and blew it toward the snowfield. The oaths they hurled at it as they chased it did nothing to slow its tumbling progress.

No wonder Kirk wanted her pack inside their tent. She'd better get to it before it suffered the same fate. With trembling knees, Darryn tried to stumble toward her tent. But it didn't work. She sank back to the turf.

She couldn't understand it. A few minutes ago, she'd been keeping up with the men. Oh, she'd realized that Yogurt had kept the pace pretty slow, but her legs had done what she'd told them. Now her mind seemed to be the only part of her body still functioning.

She began to shiver. She didn't feel cold exactly, except when a gust of wind hit her. But she couldn't stop the violent trembling of her shoulders and legs. She curled into a ball.

In a few minutes, Kirk returned and handed her a candy bar that must have weighed half a pound. "Can you eat that?"

Darryn looked at it with distaste but she began tugging at the wrap. It seemed much too hard to tear and she gave up. "No."

Kirk ripped it open for her and stuck it near her mouth. "Take a bite, Darryn," he said, his tone cajoling. "You've hit the wall. You need calories."

Darryn took a bite of...something. "Yuch!" She tried to chew it quickly to get it over with, but the lump remained heavily in her mouth. "What is this? It tastes like . . . dirt with hay mixed in."

Kirk smiled. "Something like that."

Darryn kept chewing. "I can't swallow it. It just chews."

"Try." Kirk stood.

"I can't," she said. "It wouldn't go down."

He was really frowning now. "Okay, spit it out." When she did, he pushed a lemon drop between her lips. It tasted slightly of fuzz from his pocket. "Suck that. You need sugar, quick."

Lemon sugar had never tasted so good. After a few swallows, she began to feel less shaky. "Gosh," she said. "I've never felt like that before. What does 'hit the wall' mean?"

"Ever done aerobics?"

Darryn nodded.

"That means 'with oxygen,'" Kirk said. "Lots of panting, which gives your body energy. When you exert yourself so hard that you can't get enough energy that way, your body starts to use up the glycogen stored in your muscles: that's anaerobic. When you run out of glycogen, you hit the wall."

"Sounds awful," Darryn murmured, starting to shiver again. "Feels worse."

Kirk hunkered down beside her. "What did you eat today before you got dropped off?"

Darryn bit her lip and tried to remember her life before this hike. It seemed so far away and unimportant. "I think . . ." She cast her mind back to morning. "Nothing I guess. I was kind of nervous about the trip. I had quite a bit of coffee, and I bought a cheese Danish at the airport but it wasn't very good so I threw it away after a couple of bites."

Kirk groaned. "Let's get you to the tent."

Grabbing her waist, he hauled Darryn to her feet and pulled one of her arms around his neck. The contact felt wonderful. Kirk's whole body radiated heat and Darryn wanted to turn into him and snuggle till her shivers stopped.

"Walk, Darryn," Kirk coaxed. "You remember, one foot in front of the other."

"Mmm," she said, leaning her head into his neck.

She took a step so close to his that their feet tangled, nearly tripping her.

"Oh hell." Kirk lifted her and carried her across the scree field.

Darryn heard some hoots from the other men, including an "oh la la, Kirk," from Yogurt. But Kirk ignored them, so she did also.

Depositing her in the tent, he untangled her hands from around his neck and left. She pulled her pack and Kirk's close to her and lay down, trying to stay warm. Soon, he returned with an aluminum cup containing chicken noodle soup.

"Drink this," he ordered. There was nothing cajoling about his tone this time.

Still lying on her side, Darryn swallowed a few sips of the hot liquid and began to feel better. She sat up with her back against a pack and drank some more.

"That's good," she said. "Thanks."

"How do you feel now?"

"It'd take too long to tell you everything that hurts," Darryn said.

"But better than a few minutes ago?"

"A lot better." She drained the cup.

"So don't go anorexic on me again, huh? You've got to pour in calories. As much as you can, and more."

A smile played over her lips. "If you only knew how I've longed to hear a man say those words."

Kirk frowned. "I'm serious, Darryn."

"So am *I*," Darryn said, refusing to match his solemn tone. "Believe me, no man has ever told me to gain weight."

Kirk let his eyes slide over her, reminding her how close he'd held her moments ago. She remembered the feel of his arms around her hazily, as if the experience had happened in a dream.

"Someone should have," Kirk said. "You weigh less than my pack."

"That I believe." She held the empty cup toward him.

When he seemed not to notice, she took his fingers, as he had done hers earlier, and wrapped them around the cup.

"Thanks, Kirk."

His hands didn't feel rough and callused on this side, though as she drew her fingers away she felt several scratches across the back of his hand. She looked down to see his fingers tighten around the cup. As she raised her eyes, she caught a flash of some emotion cross Kirk's face but he shuttered his expression too quickly for her to read.

He took the cup. "Pull yourself together and come out and eat dinner. You can wait until tomorrow to learn how to set up your tent, which you'll be doing every night. But you'll have to do the dishes tonight because you didn't cook." He crawled toward the opening. "Though Yogurt will no doubt take pity on you and do them for you."

"Why does that make you mad?" Darryn asked, surprisingly hurt at his withdrawal. A moment ago, she'd thought Kirk was on her side. Now she felt bereft. "I won't ask him to. I *can* do the dishes, you know."

"Yeah, but Yogurt's too much of a soft heart, or too much of a Frenchman, to let a female who's hit the wall do her own dishes. Or anything else. At least not one with eyes as blue as yours." He released a disgusted breath. "Damn but these trips are easier without women."

He left the tent before Darryn could answer, which was all right with her. She didn't really want to trade insults with the man who might have her life in his hands. Besides she hadn't thought of a crushing enough response. But she would. Given time, a little food, a little strength and she darn well would.

CHAPTER THREE

As SHE melted snow on the tiny stove to wash the few communal dishes, Darryn watched Yogurt, with Kirk and Roger, crawl up the side of the cliff like spiders. When she'd asked Kirk why they didn't use ropes, he said they were only "bouldering". Apparently that meant they wouldn't go high enough to get hurt if they fell. But it didn't look that way to Darryn.

It was the chance of bouldering that had kept Yogurt from offering to do her evening chore for her, though he'd sympathized with her vociferously, knowing how tired she was. The way his eyes had glowed when he realized there was enough light left to take Roger up on the bouldering suggestion made Darryn realize he too, just like Kirk, preferred mountains to females.

Getting the stew pot truly clean took more scrubbing than Darryn would have believed. The pot looked like it hadn't seen a scouring pad all summer. But she stuck with it, for it was the only device large enough to serve as a washbasin and she wanted it spotless.

By the time she'd finished and melted another pot of snow for face washing and teeth brushing, Darryn returned to her tent exhausted. She couldn't remember ever wanting sleep more.

As she pulled peanut butter and climbing ropes out of her pack on her way to her buried nightie and sleeping bag, she wondered what she'd use for a pillow. The way she felt, she could probably use a pointed rock and not notice. The soft light flannel of her gown felt more luscious than silk as it slithered over her body.

Just as she was snuggling into her bag, Kirk crawled into the tent. Darryn ducked under cover as quickly as she could. But not fast enough.

"What the devil do you have on?" Kirk demanded. "Sit up."

"Sit up?" Darryn snapped. "What are you, a voyeur or something?"

Sighing his already familiar sigh of impatience, Kirk gestured at the lump that was her inside the sleeping bag. "Are you wearing a nightgown?"

"Of course I am," Darryn said. "It's nighttime. I'm going to sleep. At least I am if you'll quit shouting."

"A nightgown!" Kirk groaned. He sat back on his haunches, glowering at the tent roof and uttering imprecations under his breath.

Darryn opened her eyes. "Are you going to do that all night?"

He brought his gaze to hers. He didn't look angry. But no hint of softness lightened his penetrating gray-eyed stare. "How often have you gone backpacking, Darryn? Really."

"Really...um..." She took a deep breath. "Never." Wincing at the flash of rage that darkened Kirk's face, Darryn held a palm toward him. "I knew, kind of, that I was getting in over my head. A little. But I had no idea the trip would be so...stressful."

"Stressful," Kirk repeated disgustedly. "Darryn, this trip is called 'extreme backpacking'. It's only for men who really want to test their endurance."

"Only men *would* want to do something so awful."

"Women used to come occasionally," Kirk said, sounding oddly defensive. "But...um..."

Darryn's curiosity clicked into high gear, roused by Kirk's sudden lack of decisiveness. It was the first chink she'd seen in this iron man's armor. "The women were too smart ever to do it again?"

Kirk didn't answer. "A better question," he said, "is how did *you* get signed up for it?"

Darryn looked at a seam in the roof of the tent.

"C'mon," Kirk said. "We're stuck with each other. You might as well tell me how you got us both into this."

"Well, I had to learn something about backpacking."

"And?" Kirk demanded. "I'm not the only guide in Montana."

Darryn pulled herself a little out of the bag, leaning back on her elbows. "It was my brother's fault. I knew he went backpacking with you every summer. But when I checked with Maizie, your agent, she said all your trips were full. Only my brother said he didn't know anyone else and you were the best and to call back and get on a waiting list."

"Not a waiting list for *this* trip," Kirk said emphatically. "Surely she told you what it would be like."

"I didn't exactly talk to Maizie the second time," Darryn admitted. "She was out and her assistant said there was a cancellation and I took it."

"That new kid?" Kirk said disgustedly. "Didn't he tell you what kind of trip it was?"

Darryn shook her head. But she didn't meet Kirk's eyes. She had no intention of ever telling him that she'd purposely called when she knew Maizie would be out of the office, so she could somehow charm her way on to one of Kirk's trips.

Kirk was glaring again. "Did he mention that there are six days of technical climbing on this trip? Did he tell you how many miles we mean to cover? Did he even hint that most of the trip will be above 10,000 feet? Did he—?"

"No!" Darryn yelled, sitting up and holding the sleeping bag around her. "Okay, I admit I told him I'd been backpacking but I sure didn't pretend I was Edmund Hillary. He didn't tell me any of that." She twisted the down-filled nylon in her hands. "I'm sure he didn't know." She shook a finger at Kirk. "It's my brother's fault, anyway. He's the one who—"

"I don't remember anyone named Langtry," Kirk said.

"He's my half brother," Darryn explained. "His name's Jordan West. And I'm going to kill him when I—"

"Jordan West?" Kirk erupted. "Jordan did this to me?"

Darryn eyed him nervously. "What are you talking about?"

Kirk laughed without mirth. "Nice to meet you, Princess Brat."

"Jordan told you that?" Darryn asked. "How mean."

Kirk shrugged. "He didn't say it mean."

"Oh? He always sounds mean when he says it to me." Darryn had an uncomfortable feeling she was pouting and she tried to pull in her lower lip. "How else could you say something like that?"

"Take it easy, Princess." His mouth twitched as he fought a grin that made Darryn's back teeth grind. "He just sounded like any fond older brother with a spoiled brat baby sister." His smile faded. "I guess he elected me to give you a reality lesson. Sorry you won't get a chance to kill him." He clenched his hands into fists, then slowly relaxed them. "I plan to kill him myself. With my bare hands. Did he know which trip you signed up for?"

"I don't think so." Darryn shook her head. "How could he? I didn't know myself. He's never taken it, has he?"

"Uh uh." Kirk rubbed a fist cross his whiskered chin. "Okay, I won't kill him. I'll just cripple him."

She couldn't tell if Kirk was still really angry or only kidding. She slid down in her bag and pulled it over her head. "I'm going to sleep now, Kirk."

She heard him rustling around, muttering about what he would do to Jordan if he ever laid his hands on him. In a few minutes she heard the zipper of her makeup bag opening.

She sat up abruptly, and the sleeping bag fell around her waist. "Just what do you think you're doing?"

"Everything in here is—" He looked up from the makeup tote at Darryn, sitting in her white cap-sleeved nightie and his words stopped.

The tent seemed to shrink as Kirk lowered his gaze from her eyes and the intensity of his stare increased. His chest expanded and fell. Darryn didn't need to look down to know her nipples showed through the white flannel. She folded her arms across her breasts. Kirk's eyes moved back and forth, as though tracing her bare arms. He swallowed.

Raising his gaze again, he held the tote toward her. "What is this stuff?" His voice sounded scratchy. "The bag weighs ten pounds."

Her own voice had trouble coming out. "I need it all."

"You can't possibly need it all." He studied the contents of the makeup tote as if nothing had ever interested him more. "And since I'm going to carry it—"

"Why are you going to carry my cosmetics?" Darryn asked.

Kirk continued to stare into the bag. "You can't carry anything, Darryn. You'll never make it."

"How will you fit it all in your pack?"

Kirk shrugged. "I'll take your pack, which is too darn big for you anyway. I've always wanted to try that brand."

Guilt stabbed at Darryn, remembering Kirk's comments about her pack earlier. He hated this kind and now it would weigh more than he was used to carrying—which was already more than anyone else carried. "I'll wear it," she said.

"You'll wear mine. It'll only have the two sleeping bags—a couple of pounds. If that's too much for you, I'll carry them, too."

"Kirk, you can't—"

He quit studying her makeup tote to stab a finger at her. "No one's ever gotten hurt on one of my trips,

Darryn. You do not get to be the first.'' He pulled three tall bottles out of the bag. ''What's this stuff?''

''Shampoo, conditioner, and—''

''You don't need any of it. I brought biodegradable soap. That's all you can use out here anyway.''

''Soap on my hair?'' She put a hand to her head, remembering again how little hair she had left. ''I guess it'll work.''

''Darn right. So you don't need this either.'' He took out the bar of beauty soap she'd used earlier. ''I won't ask if you've already defiled the wilderness with leftover suds.''

''Good,'' Darryn said weakly.

Kirk began hauling out makeup: foundation, blush, powder, eye shadow, mascara...

''Stop that!'' Darryn said, grabbing his hand. ''I need all that. I'd feel naked without it.'' She pointed to two other tall bottles still inside the bag. ''And if I put it on, I have to have that and that to take it off.''

Kirk regarded her, his gray eyes turning a molten silver. ''You don't have any on now, do you?''

Darryn shook her head.

''You look better this way.''

''Better?'' Darryn choked. ''You must be kidding! I've spent years learning how to—''

''You've got plenty of pink here.'' Kirk's fingers brushed across her cheek. ''And it won't streak when you sweat.''

As calloused as his fingers were, Darryn would have expected his touch to feel rough against her skin. But it didn't. Lightest goose down couldn't have touched her more gently.

For some reason, the tent seemed to have run out of oxygen. Darryn's lips opened to pull more air. ''Kirk, I don't think...'' she murmured, then stopped with no idea of what she'd started to say.

He expelled a gust of breath and jerked his hand back from her face as if something had burned him.

When the taut silence stretched on, Darryn looked up to see a ferocious frown creasing the skin between Kirk's brows. Somehow she knew it wasn't directed at her.

The olive drab tank top he'd donned for climbing stretched tight across his chest. He held the tote toward her. "You get to keep two things." He spoke as though nothing had happened between them, but the tightness in his voice betrayed him. "What are they?"

Darryn didn't need to look. "My moisturizer and my sun screen. And—"

"No ands."

"I'll carry it. Please. It's just my lip balm."

Kirk nodded shortly. "What about clothes? What can you leave behind?"

"Leave behind? What's going to happen to all this stuff?"

Kirk's eyes held hers. "Probably nothing. We'll put it all in a ditty bag and tie it in a tree. Most likely be right here when we get back. But if I've got to carry a lot of extra stuff, it'd damn well better be essential."

His forced gruffness eased the tension that had built between them. Darryn responded to it gladly, putting her hands on her hips and glaring at Kirk. "I *need* more clothes than you. I'm a woman." She bit her lip, wishing she'd chosen another phrase.

"I noticed." His right brow flicked up sardonically. "Believe me, I noticed."

"I need things you don't," she said, trying to bring the subject back to things mundane.

"Name one."

"Bras." As soon as she'd said it, Darryn's cheeks flamed but she returned his gaze resolutely.

Kirk looked uncomfortable. "And I need climbing tights, which you don't." He raised both brows. "I assume you won't be climbing with us?"

Her brief pretense at confidence vanished. "What will I do when you climb?" she asked, wondering if she'd have to hike miles around mountains the rest just climbed over.

"A couple of the others don't want to climb this year either," Kirk said. "You'll all stay in camp. Probably be good for your sore muscles."

"And my blisters."

Kirk rubbed his eyes with both hands. "Right. Blisters. You got some today?"

Darryn nodded.

"What'd you do for 'em?"

"I put Band-Aids on them."

"Great," he said with obvious irony.

"I had to, Kirk, or I couldn't sleep. They hurt too much, rubbing against the sleeping bag. And I didn't want to get the bag all icky."

"All *icky*'?" He sounded long-suffering again as he shook his head in resignation. "Let's see 'em."

"See my blisters?" Darryn shook her head firmly. "Don't be weird, Kirk."

Kirk took her shoulders. "I told you, Darryn, no one gets hurt on my trips." He clipped off the words. "Thanks to my good friend and your brother, you are in a situation that could seriously injure your health. People have lost feet from infected blisters. Now haul your feet out of that bag and take off the Band-Aids, or I'll do it for you." He tightened his grip as if he really meant to pull her out of the bag.

"Okay, okay," she cried.

Tugging down the hem of her gown, she wiggled free of the bag. As soon as she had her feet out, Darryn ripped off the Band-Aids before she had time to think about it.

Kirk grabbed her ankles and tugged and twisted till she flopped herself over into her stomach. Nervously she looked over her shoulder as he examined the backs of her heels.

"Not so bad," he said. "Only bleeding in a few places."

"That's good?"

"Could be worse," Kirk said. He began rummaging in his own pack. "I'll put some antiseptic on them. Leave them uncovered at night so they can heal. Tomorrow I'll give you some Second Skin and my neoprene socks. With luck, they won't get any worse."

"Ow!" shrieked Darryn as Kirk dabbed something burning on her right heel. "Your bedside manner leaves a lot to be desired."

"Give me the other foot, Darryn." A lopsided grin flashed briefly across his lips, lighting his deep set eyes. "And quit screaming, for God's sake. Yogurt will get a completely wrong idea."

Darryn bit back a gasp of pain as he dabbed quickly at her left heel. Relieved when he finished, she sat up and turned around, curling her knees up into her nightie and resting her arms on top of them. Kirk gave her a look of concern and fatigue.

"You're going to have to keep up, Darryn. Your pack'll weigh next to nothing. That'll make it easier but it won't stop your blisters. You'll need to watch them. I'll put antiseptic on them again tomorrow."

Darryn winced. "I've had better offers."

"I bet," Kirk surprised her by agreeing.

"But thanks, Kirk." She gave a little shrug. "I'm sorry I got us into such a mess."

He ran his eyes over her, making her feel more foolish than ever. She tucked her arms beneath her legs.

Kirk released a gusty breath. "I'll sleep in my bivi sac."

"Oh no, Kirk." Leaning forward, she grabbed his wrist. "You don't have to sleep outside." Suddenly Darryn realized she needed the reassurance of Kirk's presence. Whether it was her fault or Jordan's or that idiot at Maizie's, she'd gotten herself into a situation that scared her silly. She didn't want to be in it alone. She desperately needed another human near her to feel safe. "It's *my* fault, not yours, we're in this—"

With a quickness that startled her Kirk turned his hand beneath hers and captured her wrist in his strong fingers. "Use your head, Princess," he growled. "Grizzlies and hypothermia aren't the only dangers up here."

With a sudden tug, he jerked her toward him. She fell against his body, helplessly snarled in her nightie and the powerful arms he wrapped around her. He pressed his lips to the skin behind her temple. His stubbly chin grazed her neck as his soft lips moved toward her ear, making her pulse beat faster than it had all afternoon on the hike.

"How innocent are you, Darryn?" he whispered hoarsely. "Do you need me to show you *all* the dangers?"

Heat from his body surged into hers. It made her far too hot to shiver, so it must be trembling she was feeling. "No, I...you..." Darryn squirmed, trying to untangle herself. She closed her eyes, not wanting Kirk to see how unutterably foolish she felt. "Of course you don't need to tell me how men behave in the wild."

Kirk released her. "I'm not an animal because I like the wilderness, Brat." His voice sounded anything but steady. "But I am a man. Don't forget it."

Grabbing his sleeping bag and bivi sac, Kirk left the tent.

Darryn rolled over for perhaps the thousandth time and at last saw the colors of the tent barely illuminated by light outside. Finally she could get up. Despite her exhaustion last night, anxiety over her situation had combined with her bumpy bed to make her sleep restless.

Though Kirk obviously wasn't going to let her get killed on this hike, her inexperience might ruin it for nine others. The thought of spending three weeks with nine irritated men who wished to test themselves and couldn't because of her did not engender comfortable thoughts.

Nine irritated men, one of whom she found peculiarly attractive. That thought hadn't made sleep come easily either. Darryn almost groaned. She'd actually asked a man she'd known less than a day to stay the night in her tent. In the daylight, the realization shocked her more than ever.

What had possessed her? Doubtless, it was the isolation that had made her crave human proximity, not Kirk's enticing touch. She hoped he understood that. Even more she hoped he behaved as if he understood that, especially around the other men. If he made teasing remarks or gave her meaningful looks, it would only make an already awkward situation worse.

Darryn pulled herself out of her sleeping bag and dressed quickly. Crawling outside, she stretched, arching her body from side to side to see how much it hurt.

"Morning, Darryn."

She whirled to find Kirk beside her. She narrowed her eyes at him to see if she could find a hint of goading in his smile.

"Good morning, Kirk," she said, relieved to return his smile naturally.

"You into sunrises, too?" he asked.

"Actually, I rarely see sunrises except from the other end."

"Other end?"

"You know, when you've been out all night and the sun comes up just as you're getting home." She wiggled her shoulders. "But I'm too much into soft beds to sleep through this one."

The lightly pinking part of the sky just lit, far below them, a creek meandering out of the timber toward a large lake.

"Except, it *is* kind of beautiful in this light." Darryn sighed, longing for her sketch pad, though it probably would have ended up with her mascara in the bag of things Kirk was making her leave behind. "Look at that lake."

"Yeah," Kirk agreed. "Dawn's my favorite time."

Though Darryn had always thought of dawns the way she had mountains—as something to hear about later— she couldn't help, this moment, realizing what Kirk meant. It felt good being the only one awake, the only one looking at the sun rising over the mountain, lighting the forest and darkening the shadows against the granite cliff—as if somehow the view belonged only to her.

Kirk touched her arm and pointed toward a huge gray owl flapping away from them into the trees. The bird was twice as big as she'd ever imagined owls grew. Impulsively she stepped after it, as if wanting to follow it to its bed, then stopped feeling silly.

Kirk chuckled and opened his mouth to speak.

Darryn flicked her hand at him. "Don't say it."

His brow flicked up. "Don't say what?"

"That if I hadn't gotten up at dawn I wouldn't have seen the owl."

"Okay." His shoulders lifted in a shrug. The controlled strength in the easy movement reminded her how powerful his arms had felt around her last night. "I don't like to preach."

"Not until someone tries to defile your wilderness."

"Right." He reached into the pockets of his camp shirt. Pulling out soap and toothpaste, he handed them to her. "All biodegradable." He pointed in the direction of some thick scrubby bushes. "Back there looks private."

She gazed longingly down the mountain. "Too bad we're not down at that lake so I could take a real bath."

"Not a chance," Kirk said. "No washing and brushing within a hundred feet of a stream or two hundred feet of a lake."

"Couldn't I even swim in it?" she said plaintively.

"Sure," he laughed. "If you like hypothermia. Can't think of a better way to get it. In the height of summer, that lake only gets up to about forty-two degrees. It'd be even colder now."

"Don't like to preach, my foot," Darryn sniffed, turning toward the bushes.

Kirk grabbed her arm and pulled her back to face him. "I just want people to enjoy the wilderness as much as I do."

"I bet you really don't." She tugged gently to free her arm. "Anyone who liked it as much as you would try to live in it too, the way you do. If it began to fill up with other wilderness freaks, you wouldn't like it at all."

He gave her a curious look, a mixture of surprise and acknowledgment. "That's true. But there's an awful lot of room up here. I wouldn't mind convincing a *few* other people it's the best place on earth." He looked past her into the distance. "I thought I had once, but I was wrong."

Something remote in his tone sent a quiver across Darryn's shoulders. "What happened, Kirk? Was it a woman?"

Kirk stiffened and he seemed to pull away from her. "Forget it."

"But you sound so—"

"I said, forget it!"

"Yes *sir*, Mr. Storm." Darryn whirled again and began walking toward the bushes.

"Darryn."

She ignored him and kept walking. She heard a rustle and he fell into step beside her.

"Want to stop and talk to me," he asked, "or shall I follow you all the way there?"

Darryn stopped in her tracks. "Yes?" She made her voice brisk and impatient.

Kirk gave her a rueful look. "I'm sorry about last night. I didn't mean to act so...lecherous."

"Oh?" Darryn asked, her tone haughty enough to make Kirk wince. "You mean you do that sort of thing by accident?"

"Of course not." His frown deepened. "It's just been ... I just..."

Hoping she looked disdainful, Darryn pursed her lips and raised her brows. Actually she was trying not to laugh. Kirk's total command of the wilderness intimidated her so that she couldn't help enjoying his discomfiture now. Her triumph lasted only a moment.

Kirk cupped her chin in his palm, forcing her to meet his angry gray eyes. "Princess Brat is right. You change from one to the other so fast I can't keep up. I'd like to spank the brat and... I won't even mention what I'd like to do to the princess." He released her. "But I won't do either one. What happened last night won't happen again. Count on it."

Darryn bit her lip. He'd effectively stilled her desire to laugh. "I'm very glad to hear that," she said, her quaky voice probably telling Kirk more than she wanted to about how much he affected her. "I'll certainly sleep easier knowing I'm safe from your unwanted advances."

As she strode toward the bushes, she heard Kirk's quiet voice behind her. "I'll melt you a pot of wash water, Princess."

CHAPTER FOUR

KIRK shook his head as Darryn reached for the pot of coffee to refill her cup. "You'll regret it."

"I will?" She stared longingly at the pot. "Not as much as I'll regret caffeine withdrawal."

"He's right, Darryn," Alex said. "Today's hike is the worst. And we only stop once."

"Your heart rate'll get high enough without more added stimulants," Kirk said. "Besides..."

Yogurt gave her a sympathetic look. "Being the man has some advantages, little one."

Darryn looked around at the group. None of the men who had taken this trip before seemed eager for today's exertions. Yogurt, she realized now, was the only repeater who had drunk more than one cup of coffee. "What do you all know that I don't?" she asked.

"It does seem a little somber, Kirk," Roger said. "What's up?"

Kirk shut off the fuel valve on the stove. "Today we get used to the altitude. I'll lead as fast as I can. We'll go off trail whenever we can without damaging fragile ground cover. It's just a day hike, so you don't need to take your pack, unless you want to. If you do, unless you've really kept in shape all year, I'd suggest you only fill it halfway." He aimed a thumb at Alex's tent that had blown over yesterday. "Be sure to leave some weight in your tents to help stabilize them."

"How far do you plan to drag us?" Darryn asked.

"Better you do not know," Yogurt said.

"He's right," Kirk said. "Just follow and concentrate on keeping up. Everyone take a bottle of Kool-Aid and bottle of Gaterload. I'll bring the food. I don't want to hear complaints, unless someone has any of the

41

symptoms of altitude sickness we talked about. That I want to hear about fast."

Will stood and pressed his fists into the small of his back. "You'd better wear earplugs if you don't want to hear us complain."

Kirk grinned. "Okay," he said. "Just don't attack my parentage."

The men laughed and moved toward their tents to get ready. Darryn stared after them, wondering if it was her parentage they'd be attacking by the end of the day.

Kirk's hand on her elbow urged her toward her tent. "Get me your water bottles, Darryn. I'll carry your drinks."

"I can carry *something*, Kirk," she said, wondering if that were true.

"Not today. C'mon, I'll give you my neoprene socks."

Darryn stood her ground. "The others will see that you're carrying everything for me."

"So what? They'd let me carry theirs if I offered." Kirk quit urging her toward the tent and stepped in front of her. "Darryn, if you get through this day, it'll be a miracle. You don't need one extra ounce of weight to slow you down. I figure Yogurt'll have to quit halfway and bring you back to camp anyway." He studied her. "You probably shouldn't even go, except if you don't it'll be ten times worse for you later."

Resentment suddenly hit Darryn like a blow. She had taken all the condescension she could from this man. She wasn't completely out of shape. She did aerobics every morning and lifted weights twice a week. Being a man didn't give him *that* much advantage. So he could go to the bathroom on the trail easier than she. Big deal!

She poked him hard in the chest. "I'll keep up with you today, Mr. Storm."

Kirk was looking at her contemplatively. "Maybe I'll ask Yogurt to stay with you and just take you on a short hike."

"Didn't you hear me?" she asked angrily. "I said I'd keep up with you!"

He raised that infuriating brow. "You think so?"

Stubborn pride filled Darryn. "Darn right. It's a promise." *A vow* she decided to herself.

"You don't know what you're saying." He shrugged. "But if you come even close, you'll probably manage the rest of the expedition without much trouble."

"Really?"

"Really." He glanced down at her still slippered feet, a grin tugging at his lips. "But I think you'll find it easier if you wear boots." When he met her eyes again, he looked more serious. "Since you're so determined, Darryn, I won't try to make the hike any easier today. The other guys, they swear about it a lot, but it's what they come for. To push themselves to the limit."

"Push all you want, Kirk."

He gave her a long look, not quite frowning, but very intent. "Don't get hurt, Darryn. If you feel anything dangerous, let me know immediately."

"Kirk, stop it," she said indignantly. "No matter what you think, I'm not some pampered princess who rides everywhere in a sedan chair. I'll make it. On my own. And I'll carry my own water."

Worry clashed with respect on Kirk's face. "It's probably dumb to let you go," he said. "But I guess if you really think you can make it, I'll believe you till I see otherwise." He gestured toward the tent again. "Let's get the socks, and *I'll* carry your drinks."

With a flip of her hands, Darryn gave in. "Stubbornest man alive," she muttered, heading for the tent.

Within an hour, Darryn knew letting Kirk carry her water was the smartest thing she'd ever done. The dumbest was declaring, promising, *vowing*, she would keep up on the trail.

That had *been her promise, hadn't it*? she argued to herself as she broke another fingernail crawling over a huge boulder that Kirk had merely stepped onto. On the

trail? Hadn't she only promised to keep up *on the trail*?
No, she groaned mentally—she hadn't enough breath to
groan aloud. She knew darn well her promise had been
to keep up no matter where Kirk took them.

Jumping down from the boulder, she tried to raise her
leg high enough to climb over another dead tree in their
path. Things hadn't been too bad on the trail. Oh, her
lungs had ached and her mouth had run out of moisture
in a few minutes. But climbing over this dead fall in a
forest so thick she could barely see thirty feet ahead
turned her legs to heavy wooden blocks she could hardly
lift. And the hike had scarcely begun.

Her head pounded as the blood rushed past her
temples. She wanted to tell Kirk she needed another
drink, but her breath came too fast to speak. He must
have heard the increased raspiness in her panting. Or
perhaps he simply knew enough time had passed for her
to need fluid.

As they dropped back onto the relative comfort of the
trail, Kirk handed her the bottle of carbohydrate replacement without slowing a step. Darryn wanted to
laugh at the thought she could possibly consider this
trail—this narrow, rocky, rutted, precipitous switchback
trail—comfortable. Worst of all as far as Darryn was
concerned, it led steeply *down*hill. Not only did that
make her knees tremble like unset Jell-O, but it also
meant she'd have to hike back *up* this mountain before
she got back to her tent.

Of course, she was far too breathless and thirsty to
waste air actually laughing. Besides—she glanced quickly
out again across the deep canyon—she might lose her
footing and tumble off, sliding down the mountainside
to that rock slab far below. She almost wished they'd
climb back into the thick tumber, where at least she could
cling to trees when the going got this steep.

Kirk had insisted she walk right behind him so he could
keep her from total collapse. But that gave her small
comfort. For he'd worn her pack, loaded with every-

thing of his *and* hers that he would have to carry the next three weeks. He had to get used to the new pack and added weight sometime, he'd told her. Now every time she raised her eyes and saw his powerful legs pushing ahead, she felt a stab of guilt. Most of the time though, she kept her eyes on her feet or she stumbled.

After a gulp or two she returned the bottle to Kirk. She had to quit thinking about how much every part of her hurt. She had to simply turn herself into a robot and make her limbs and lungs work as if they belonged to someone else.

She watched her thighs rise and fall, hoping to forget the pain. She tried to detach herself from the sound of her labored breathing, from the feel of sweat sticking her hair to her scalp.

Nothing worked.

Then Kirk turned off the trail again, this time into a dry streambed. Darryn would have cried but she didn't want to waste precious body moisture on tears. Her ankles throbbed as they wobbled uphill over the uneven rocks.

Kirk was right. She couldn't make it.

As she gathered the breath to tell him so, Will swore roughly, cursing Kirk as a sadistic martinet the equal of Captain Bligh. The others joined in, expressing all their pain and exhaustion as wrath at Kirk, and those who had begotten him, and Yogurt and Montana. Kirk returned their gibes with no more seriousness but equal vulgarity. Yogurt threw in several French phrases that could have been directed at any of them.

Darryn was stunned! They all sounded as tired as she, even Kirk. His voice came out harsh with thirst. Deep gasps for air separated his oaths.

His pain gave her hope. If he wanted to stop as much as she did, then maybe this hike of his wouldn't kill her after all. Lunch had to come sooner or later. She'd make it just till lunch, she decided. Then if her legs absolutely refused to take another step, she'd ask Yogurt to drag her back to camp.

A lifetime later, Darryn collapsed on a gravel bar at the foot of a beautiful waterfall. This time of year its flow was small, but the water fell a hundred feet, plummeting over rocks that scattered the stream out in huge watery fans that she could see through to the lichen covered granite behind.

After a long exhausted stare, Darryn lost interest. She wanted only to close her eyes and lie here forever, letting the mist slowly cool her. When she was completely cool, they could bury her.

"Don't lie down, Darryn. You'll cramp up."

Only Kirk would say something so unnatural at such a time. No one in her right mind would take him seriously. Darryn ignored him.

"Did you hear me, Darryn?"

She licked her lips with no effect. "What you said was so ridiculous I assumed I hallucinated it."

"Hallucinated?" Kirk demanded. How could he speak so normally? "Are you having—?"

She sat up, bumping into Kirk's chest as he hunkered over her. "You really are a sadist, aren't you, Kirk?"

A broad smile spread across his face. "I guess you're all right."

"All right? Not a chance. I think I died two hours ago."

He handed her a bottle of Gaterload. "Two hours ago, we'd just started."

"That sounds right," Darryn said, gulping greedily. "Dead since the third or fourth step."

"Want some lunch?"

"Pheasant under glass?" she asked.

"How about peanut butter and jelly?"

Darryn hated peanut butter, especially with jelly. But with her thirst slaked, the thought of food, any food, sounded delicious. "I'll take four sandwiches."

"How about two sandwiches and a bag of trail mix?"

"Trail mix," Darryn sighed. "A culinary delight."

Kirk grinned and went to get the food. Darryn rubbed her quadriceps and tried to stand. She felt better than yesterday at the camp, yet she believed they'd walked farther, certainly over rougher terrain. Maybe Kirk's system of drinking calories and carbohydrates worked.

She didn't want to admit how good she felt. Not that "good" described any part of her. Her feet burned, her legs screamed with pain, even her arms ached. Her throat and chest felt raw from all her panting. The knowledge that this excruciating day was only half over hurt her mind as much as her boots hurt her feet.

But she was still with them. No one had had to pick her up beside the trail and carry her back to her tent. That made her feel better than she'd ever have imagined.

Of course, most of the men had carried packs at least partially full, and she hadn't carried a thing. In fact, as Kirk's unattended pack lying on the grass caught her eye, Darryn remembered the sweatshirt and windbreaker he'd untied from around her waist earlier and added to his already heavy load. He hadn't seemed to notice the extra weight, but she had felt the added guilt with every step. Though she *had* felt more comfortable without all that heat around her middle.

After splashing a little icy water in her face, Darryn headed toward the bank, determined to retrieve her sweatshirt and carry *something* on this hike. That little compartment on top, where Kirk stowed the first aid kit, was where he'd stuffed her clothes. She groped inside but couldn't find anything of hers.

Straightening, she came eye to eye with Kirk. "Trying to stuff yourself in the pack, Princess?" Kirk handed her a bag of nuts and dried fruit. "It's not a sedan chair."

She gave him a sarcastic smile at his weak joke and took the sandwiches he proffered. "I just wanted to lighten your load, Kirk."

"Then work on staving off collapse this afternoon," he said, "so I don't have to carry you back."

Darryn glared at him as he delivered lunch to the others. She wondered what feat of heroism she'd have to perform to convince Kirk she wasn't a total incompetent.

Yogurt joined her on a rock while she ate. "A poor substitute for yogurt, *n'est-ce pas*?" He chewed a bite of his sandwich.

"Is that why you're called 'Yogurt'?"

"*Naturellement.* When I first came to your country, I wanted only to climb rocks. I did not have much money and I knew no English. French yogurt was the only thing I recognized in the grocery market—except your odd cuts of beef, which I could not afford, and your bread, which is inedible." His lips curled. "Until I met Kirk and found a way to acquire a living wage from the climbing, I ate nothing else."

"How did you meet Kirk?" Darryn asked. "His trips aren't cheap."

"Indeed not," Yogurt agreed, dusting crumbs off his fingers onto the wax paper that had wrapped his sandwich. Carefully, he wadded the paper with the crumbs still inside. "But the world of climbing is small. I simply stood at the base of difficult climbs offering belays, and I met many climbers. They taught me English, yes?"

"Kind of," Darryn giggled. "Don't you have any family, Yogurt?"

"But of course." The sparkle that had never left his eyes since Darryn met him, dulled. "My son and daughter are in the Himalayas, conquering mountains I am too old to attempt."

"Isn't that dangerous?"

"Ah *oui*, little one." Yogurt gestured expansively. "But so exciting."

"And their mother?"

"She does not find it so exciting." He stared at the water cascading down the rocks. "And me...she has not found anything exciting about me since I quit my government job and introduced our children to the Alps.'' Yogurt stood. ''But she is only a woman, yes?'' He pointed toward the closest range of granite peaks. ''What woman can compare with that?''

Yogurt's gesture drew Darryn's eyes toward the starkly rugged range. They did not tower, these Beartooths. They were too barren and harsh looking, too huge, to merely tower. They loomed over the helpless infinitesimal humans who dared to enter them.

She tried to visualize giving up a soft bed to sleep in such a place. Tried to imagine giving up the security of a comfortable job to tie one's body precariously to thousand foot rock walls.

She shuddered. ''I don't understand.''

''No, little one, you do not.'' He shook his head. ''How could you? I do not understand it myself. Climbing is not a sport. It is a passion. The grand passion. One has it or one does not.''

''Sounds like an obsession to me,'' Darryn said.

Yogurt wasn't offended. ''Perhaps.'' He offered her a hand up. ''Do you wish privacy before the hike back?''

No, she wished for a two hour nap, but she supposed she wasn't going to get it. Still this logy feeling assailing her must be attacking all the others too, maybe even Kirk. Surely he'd take that into consideration this afternoon.

She should have known better, Darryn thought later, than to expect consideration when hiking with the Marquis de Sade. But she refused to give in. She panted and sweated and downed Gaterload till she thought she would float away. But she didn't think of her exhaustion and pain, she thought only of the wonderful satisfaction she'd felt lying at the foot of the waterfalls. She would feel that again when they got back to camp. She would feel it again if it killed her.

Cresting a steep hill behind Kirk's annoyingly strong legs, Darryn's lowered gaze caught sight of three pinecones. ''Oh thank heaven,'' she murmured.

"What did you say?" Kirk asked without slowing down or turning around.

"I said..." Darryn gasped "...thank heaven we're...almost home."

"Whoa," Kirk called, holding up a hand. He spun around to face her, his eyes alight with curiosity. "What makes you think we're almost home?"

As the men groaned with relief at this unexpected rest, Darryn leaned against a tree and bent over, trying to catch her breath enough to speak. Her words came out broken by pants.

"Those...pinecones. Three of...them together...like that." She gestured vaguely with her hand. "Especially that one...that's all opened up...by a chipmunk."

Kirk stared at her as if she'd grown two heads, yet a grudging respect warmed his expression. "Pinecones?" he asked, his voice oddly hopeful.

"There." She pointed at the triangular configuration. "A chipmunk was eating...that one this...morning."

"Actually, it was a ground squirrel," said Kirk. "I saw him. We scared him off." His voice sounded less raspy than Darryn's, though his chest expanded and fell rapidly. "I didn't think anyone else noticed, you were all complaining so loudly then."

"The light..." Darryn waved at the trees overhead "...was different then. It's...coming the other...way now. The cones were in...shadow this morning. So...it must be...much later now. We must...be almost done."

With one finger, Kirk pushed his cap to the back of his head. "I'm impressed, Princess. I really am."

A chorus of voices seconded Kirk's statement and accused him of misjudging her. Yogurt, who had more air than the others, was especially insulting. But no one had enough breath to give a long speech in Darryn's defense.

"Kirk..." Darryn straightened up. "Don't tell...me you're impressed... Tell me...we're almost done."

"What made you notice?" Kirk asked, his tone echoing an esteem he'd previously saved only for the men. "Are you an environmentalist or something?"

Darryn shook her head. "A commercial artist." Kirk's unwavering stare was beginning to make her feel defensive. "I notice...what I see."

Kirk held up both hands as if conceding a point. "You certainly do. Who would dispute it?"

"*Are* we...almost home?" she asked.

He regarded her a moment. "So you really don't know where you are." He sounded disappointed. "You just know you were here this morning."

Something about his tone challenged Darryn. She drew her shoulders back and spoke without panting. "I know we're close to camp."

At this statement, silence fell. A moment before, Darryn hadn't particularly noticed the noises from the men. But suddenly their heavy breathing and murmurings quieted. The noises of their packs rustling and their water bottles opening and closing ceased.

Kirk's broad smile and devilishly crinkling eyes issued the challenge even before he verbalized it. "Can you lead us home, Miss Langtry?"

"Lead?" Darryn cocked her head. "Do I get to set the pace?"

"Go for it, Darryn," yelled Alex.

"Do it," Roger said, "please!"

"Set the pace hell!" Kirk exclaimed. "If you can do it, I'll do the dishes for you the rest of the trip."

"Not a chance, Kirk" Darryn said, her voice finally coming out near normal. She took the bottle of Kool-Aid from him. "I saw how you do the dishes and it's disgusting. I need to use that pot for washing." She gulped liquid.

Kirk laughed. "Okay, I'll do your cooking."

She eyed him. "Did you cook that stuff we ate last night?"

Kirk's smile was beginning to look forced. "Yes," he said.

"No deal," said Darryn.

This time, Kirk didn't laugh at all, but the others did. Especially Yogurt. "*Merci bien*, little one."

Kirk put his fists on his hips. "Okay, lady. What do you want?"

"*You* set up my tent every night."

Kirk glared at her, and she knew she'd won. He couldn't back down from this deal now, not with everyone listening. "Okay. But remember. If you go astray, I'm not going to tell you. Every false step you take will lead nine tired hungry men *away* from food and rest." He put out his hand. "Deal?"

Darryn chewed at her bottom lip. Nervously, she looked over her shoulder at the men.

"We'll follow you anywhere," Roger said.

She stared down the trail ahead of them. It could hardly be called a trail. She saw only rocks and pine needles along a steeply sloping hillside, nothing like yesterday's boulevard of hard packed earth. Still, in the fading light, she could see shadows of the marks they'd made this morning in the loose dirt, places where the pine needles had been shoved thickly together by a booted foot.

She grabbed Kirk's hand. "Deal."

Before she had time to think about what she'd gotten herself into, Darryn started forward. She didn't go nearly as fast as Kirk, but she didn't hear any complaints about that. She'd seen which direction to start before she quit arguing with Kirk, but she feared each step would take her to a spot she didn't remember that revealed no hints of this morning's trek.

But it didn't happen. She remembered those flat rocks because the markings on them looked like bear paws. There they were, all six of them. She remembered the white boulder that looked like limestone because she'd broken her fingernail on it. In fact, Darryn leaned forward staring at the rock, there it still was with a bit of her blood.

How, gross!

The clues never ran out. She didn't realize how close she'd gotten until the men walked past her, heading for their tents. She looked up and saw camp not far away through the trees.

"You made it, Princess," Kirk said, holding out his hand in congratulation. "Gimme five."

"I don't believe it," Darryn said, limply slapping his hand. "That can't be our camp."

Kirk's smile was almost as genuine as when he looked at the mountains. "Why not?"

Darryn pursed her lips, pretending to look dismayed. "I was sure our camp had a hot tub," she said. "I thought about it all afternoon."

Kirk's smile didn't fade but he didn't seem very amused. "It's too late to convince me you're an airhead, Darryn, so don't try." He shrugged. "Spoiled maybe. Muleheaded as, um..."

"As a mule?" she suggested.

"A mule," he agreed. "But up here," he put his hand gently on top of her head, "are brains." He slid his palm down her scalp to the back of her head, holding her gaze to his. "And the eyes of an eagle." He cocked his head as if studying her eyes. "Though I've never seen an eagle with eyes quite that blue."

Darryn took his wrist and pulled his hand from her head. Of course, she just meant to pull his hand down and then release him. That's the only reason she'd touched him. But somehow she didn't. She stood holding his wrist in both her hands, feeling his pulse beneath her fingers.

"When did you ever see an eagle this close?"

Kirk's lips quirked as though they wanted to smile but didn't quite make it. "I've seen them close," he said, "but never held hands with one."

He probably meant she ought to let him go. They'd already decided this kind of thing wasn't smart. His pulse quickened, and she wondered what he thought of her holding his hand this way. He didn't make her wonder long.

"Never seen one either..." his voice sounded rough again, as it had on the hike—well, not *exactly* as it had on the hike "...put together like this." He ran his thumb over her lips, from one side to the other, tugging them slightly apart. He leaned closer. "Never even imagined wanting to kiss one of those sharp beaks."

Now, Darryn thought as his warmth closed on her, now is the time to let go of his wrist: let go and step back. Instead she found herself squeezing his wrist harder than ever as his mouth came down on the lips he'd parted.

She'd never kissed a man who thought so little of shaving. Though his whiskered jaw felt scratchy against her skin, it didn't distract her from the kiss. In fact, she barely noticed its rough masculinity at all. She barely noticed anything besides Kirk's mouth, seeming to take hers inside, his tongue tracing the line of her lips, urging them to open wider. And his pulse. Beneath her fingertips, she felt the steady throb begin to pound, faster and harder and much more erratically.

He put his other hand behind her waist, pulling her toward him. Without much strength, he tugged at the hand she held. Darryn wouldn't release him. She held tight to his wrist as she leaned up and into his kiss. Kirk crushed her to him, pressing their tangled hands between their chests.

He slid his hand up her spine to the back of her head. Gripping her there, he deepened the kiss. Darryn's thoughts began to swirl out of control. As she opened her mouth, she could no longer remember what she'd thought unwise about kissing Kirk.

With the tight band of his arm holding her where he wanted her, his delving tongue caressing the recesses of her mouth, Darryn quit trying to think. Feeling was more than enough. She squirmed closer, wanting to feel more.

Small whimpers came from her, surprising her. Her hands, trapped between their bodies, felt her heart and Kirk's as a cacophony of beats, so loud she was sure the others could hear it in their tents.

The thought of tents reminded her, gradually, of her surroundings. Dear heaven, she hoped none of the men could see them through the trees.

With more effort than she'd have believed necessary, Darryn drew back. "Your heart," she murmured, resting her head against his chest.

"Mm?" Kirk sighed, leaning his cheek on top of her head.

"Isn't there some aerobic rule about heart rates?" she said with as much voice as she could coax out of her lungs.

Kirk chuckled. "You think we're exceeding it?"

"By a mile." She took a few breaths. "There's that other rule too."

Darryn released Kirk's hand and tried to stand straight. He slipped his now freed arm around her waist and slid his other arm softly down her back to link with it, forming a warm cordon around her body, holding her to him.

"What rule is that?"

She quit fighting him and relaxed in his embrace. "The one about how dumb this is in all this isolation. You remember, the one about what an animal you are in the wilderness."

Kirk remained silent but he stiffened. He didn't pull away or release her, but the momentary vulnerability she'd felt in him vanished. Without moving, he seemed to withdraw.

"At least we're not in the tent," she said.

Kirk took her face between his palms. "Darryn, you know that door on the tent?"

"Yes."

"It's got a zipper, not a dead bolt lock." He shook his head. "You're right. This is dumb."

Darryn's hurt must have shown on her face. Kirk instantly softened.

"I didn't say it wasn't nice, Darryn. It's too damn nice."

Kirk drew a long breath and took his hands from her face. Putting them behind him, like a kid in a candy store, he stepped back. Without any contact between them, Darryn felt a chill shiver down her spine.

She looked at the determined set of his shoulders. "This is only the second day, Kirk."

He rolled his eyes "Don't remind me." Then he shook his head firmly, as if trying to clear it of unwanted thoughts. "No, Darryn, don't be ridiculous. We're adults with normal urges, but not ones we can't control. If you want me in your tent, just say so. Believe me, I won't mind. If you want me out, then tell me that. I'm not a rutting grizzly, for God's sake. I won't have any problem sleeping alone. I've done it for years."

Darryn thought he protested too much. Was he trying to convince her or himself? Of course, she didn't fear for a minute that Kirk would invade her tent, unasked, to force himself on her.

But she'd also had enough experience with the human urges Kirk mentioned to believe that the rest of the trip would be easy for either of them. Not that she had tons of experience with kisses as passionate as Kirk's. In fact, when she thought about it, she'd never before in her life experienced a kiss like Kirk's.

"Well?" Kirk demanded, planting his fists on his hips.

Darryn realized he expected *her* to make this decision. Well, it was easy enough to make with a man she'd only known a day. Wasn't it? She ran her eyes over him, realizing he didn't look nearly as scruffy as she'd thought the first time she'd seen him. In fact, remembering the way that unshaved jaw had felt against her skin, he looked rather appealing.

Appealing, Darryn? she moaned to herself. *Have you lost your mind?*

"Darryn!" Kirk exploded.

"Oh no you don't, Kirk Storm," Darryn began angrily, then realized she was only angry with him for attracting her and arousing her and then behaving like a gentleman. Still this was a two person decision and she would not be forced to make it herself. "I trust you to do the right thing, Kirk."

Kirk made a noise that Darryn thought sounded very much like a rutting grizzly and strode away. The fluid motions of his powerful body disappearing in the dusk only confirmed what Darryn already knew: she definitely had gotten herself into big, big trouble.

CHAPTER FIVE

IN HER TENT, Darryn massaged her throbbing feet, thankful again that she'd brought her slippers, no matter what Kirk thought of them. If she had to force her feet back inside those boots tonight, she'd need amputation by morning.

Curling on top of her sleeping bag, she shoved her jacket into a pillow beneath her head. She'd worked darned hard today, she had earned a nap... and a lot of food. No matter how foul Kirk's concoction for dinner, she would eat three helpings.

Kirk rattled the fly of the tent. "Madam chef?" he called through the screen. "You're on."

"Chef?" Darryn blinked herself fully awake. "You mean cook? Me?"

Kirk unzipped the screen and ducked to look inside at her. "You insisted on it, if I remember." He looked stern and unyielding.

He must be angry because she hadn't invited him to share her tent for the rest of the trip. Though that didn't seem like him. Surely he hadn't expected it. She'd only known him two days. Could that be his usual practice on these trips? Jordan hadn't given her the impression that Kirk was... well, the sort to hop from bed to bed— or sleeping bag to sleeping bag.

Perhaps Kirk was acting remote simply to put emotional distance between them. After all, he too had seemed to realize that a repeat of their passionate encounter after the hike wouldn't be wise.

Whatever his reasons, Darryn missed the warmth and friendliness he'd shown her earlier.

"I didn't know I had to cook *tonight*," she began. Then added hurriedly, "Okay, okay," as Kirk opened his mouth to begin what looked like a lecture she'd already heard once too often. She crawled outside and stretched, rubbing her hands up and down the small of her back. "Just tell me that tomorrow we get to lie in our tents till noon."

"Tomorrow?" Kirk's stern look faded. "Tomorrow we climb." His eyes glowed with another kind of passion, one that had nothing to do with her, as he gazed at the cliff sheltering the tents. "Did you think we hiked to this face for nothing? Four pitches of five eight or higher." The sigh of pleasure he expelled reminded Darryn of her father's sighs after a difficult but successful surgery.

She thought of watching these men she'd come to like scaling a cliff that looked to her very nearly vertical. "I don't think I can watch."

"Then hide in your tent, Darryn." As if with an effort, Kirk dragged his gaze away from the rock face, looking completely baffled that someone could feel so negative about the sport he loved. "Because nothing could keep us from it." He gave her a gentle push toward the cook stove. "Now feed us, woman."

"Right," Darryn said, glad to take her eyes from that threatening wall. "A hearty meal for the condemned."

At the stove, Kirk handed Darryn a list of recipes. "We have supplies to make any of these," he said. "You can experiment if you want, but don't get carried away. The food has to last three weeks."

Darryn glanced at the list of one pot meals, called "glops". "Perfect name for what we ate last night," she murmured.

Kirk bristled. "It contained all the food groups, everything you needed to make that hike today."

"All the food groups?" Darryn said. "Kirk, I think you misunderstood the nutritionists. You're supposed to get all the food groups in one day, not in one pot."

"Fine, Princess," he growled. "Cook whatever you want, but make sure we get what we need and don't use up two weeks supplies in one night." He walked away.

Darryn grinned at his retreating back. It obviously irritated Kirk that his legendary competence in the back country did not extend to cooking.

As she began digging through the supplies, however, her sympathy for the task increased. It wouldn't be easy to produce something even edible, much less delicious, with instant mashed potatoes and dehydrated vegetables. Still she didn't need to prepare everything in the same pan.

At that altitude over such tiny stoves, "instant" food took quite a while to cook. Darryn used the time to prepare biscuits, with powdered buttermilk and some of the butter she found. She baked them over the pots of stew and mashed potatoes by inverting the pot lids and covering them with foil to make tiny ovens.

Though the meal didn't approach culinary perfection, the men raved about it as though they'd discovered a five star restaurant in the wilderness.

"Darryn," Will said, snatching the last biscuit just as Yogurt reached for it. "I'll carry your pack every day, if you can keep Kirk away from the kitchen for the rest of the trip."

"And, little one," Yogurt said, looking mournfully at the biscuit Will was relishing, "I will carry *you* if you simply agree to make biscuits for every meal."

Darryn laughed though she had an uneasy feeling the gibes at Kirk were hitting a sore spot.

"Not a chance," she said. "Cooking rotates, and don't give me that baloney about a woman's place. Anyone with half a mind—and even men have *that* much, don't they?—can learn to make biscuits. Besides you're all so hungry you would have eaten baked shoe leather."

"We had that last night," Alex said. "Let's see...who was cooking then?"

"Funny," Kirk snapped. "It's your night to do the dishes, Alex. Why don't you get started? I'm going to do the route finding for tomorrow."

With that, he rose and strode away from the group toward the rock face. Dismayed, Darryn watched him go. The teasing had all been good-natured. Kirk did everything so well, the men obviously found it a relief, just as she did, to discover something they did better than he. But she couldn't understand why he cared. No one took Kirk's trips for the food.

Darryn started to follow him then sank back onto her rock seat. They'd agreed, sort of, that being alone together presented risks. Chasing after him into the dusk, with no one else around to curb the intensity of what she now recognized as a strong attraction to Kirk, didn't seem wise.

"Go ahead, little one," Yogurt said softly.

"What are you talking about, Yogurt?" Guiltily, she glanced around and saw that the others had left them alone.

Yogurt smiled, his eyes crinkling and sparkling with his unbridled sex appeal. Darryn wondered how his wife could have left him, even if he did spend most of his life on a mountain. "You wish to go talk to Kirk . . . go." He gave an expressive French shrug. "You do not commit a crime by liking Kirk, little one. I like him too."

"It's not the same, Yogurt."

"*Grace a Dieu*," Yogurt said, "I should hope not."

"It's not a good idea."

"*Vraiment*? Please explain to me why not. To me it sounds like a magnificent idea."

Darryn couldn't help laughing at Yogurt's suggestive grin but she sobered quickly. "Why do you say that? Does Kirk always . . ." She hesitated, knowing this was none of her business. "Does he . . . every trip I mean, find a woman to share his—?"

"Never, little one." Yogurt spoke without humor now. "One time, long ago, and never since."

"Never since?" Darryn said. "He must have . . . um, really loved her."

"That is for Kirk to say."

Darryn picked up a smooth rock and began turning it over in her hands. "Did you know her, Yogurt?"

He nodded.

Darryn looked back at her rock. "I suppose she was fit and strong and loved the mountains and could climb sheer faces?"

Yogurt snorted. "She liked those things, yes. She liked the comforts of civilization more." He gave another expressive shrug. "Personally, from the moment I put my eyes on her, I did not like her. I did not think she would make Kirk happy, though he seemed to disagree...for a time. If you want to ask him about it, he is over there by the face." Yogurt waved vaguely in the direction of the cliff.

"I know where he is, Yogurt," Darryn said. "I have no intention of asking him things that are none of my business. Which is undoubtedly what he'd tell me."

"No?" Yogurt said, the smile back in his voice and on his lips. "You ask me instead?"

"I was worried about him," Darryn said defensively. "He seemed upset by all the teasing. Why does he care how well he cooks?"

Yogurt stood. "As I said, he is over there. Go ask him. I am going to bed so I will be fresh for the climb."

Darryn rose too. "That's probably the best idea," she said. "I think I'll go to bed too."

"Oh, *bien sur*," Yogurt said sardonically. "Tell Kirk I said good night."

Darryn gave him what she hoped was a quelling look and walked toward her tent. As she neared it, the sight of Kirk standing alone by the sheer face tugged on her heartstrings. He looked strong, standing there with his back to the tents, and determined. But next to the wall of rock rising hundreds of feet above him, he appeared tiny. And so alone.

Darryn would argue with anyone Jordan's notion that she was a spoiled brat. But she would willingly admit that she was adored. All her life, no matter how angry she made them, she had never doubted Jordan's love or her mother's or, especially, Daddy's.

Because of their love, Darryn never felt truly alone.

She walked toward Kirk, wondering about his family. Had he ever felt surrounded by love too, as every kid should? Why was he so alone? Did he really choose it? Or did he get stuck with it somehow? And why did he struggle so hard to maintain it?

With her eyes on Kirk instead of the ground, Darryn suddenly stepped onto the snowfield in her slippered feet. "Ooo," she squealed as bits of slushy snow slithered along her soles. "Brrr."

Kirk spun around to watch her hopping ungracefully on one foot as she shook snow from a slipper. In a few long strides, he was beside her and took her arm above the elbow to steady her. "I should have known," he muttered.

"Should have known what?" She grimaced as she put the damp slipper back on her foot.

"That it was you sneaking toward me across the scree field."

"I wasn't sneaking," Darryn protested.

"Probably not." Kirk urged her toward the tent. "It just sounded like sneaking. I should have figured it was slippers instead of boots crunching on the stones."

"It's not easy walking on these loose rocks in slippers, you know."

"No doubt." Kirk kept his hand around her arm as they walked. "That's why most of us wear boots in the mountains, Princess. What did you want up here anyway? Planning to climb with us tomorrow after all?"

"Good heavens, no!" Darryn shuddered at the thought. "I just wanted to ask you something."

"Ask away," Kirk said easily. Thirty minutes contemplating tomorrow's climb had obviously lightened his mood.

But Darryn couldn't get the words out. She sensed her question would probe parts of Kirk he wished to keep private.

"What is it, Darryn?"

"I just wondered why you..." She hesitated. "You seemed so upset by all the teasing. Why do you care that you're not... the galloping gourmet of the wilderness?" His grip tightened around her upper arm, almost painfully.

Kirk kept walking, pulling Darryn with him.

She stepped in front of him to stop him. "That's not why these men come with you, you know, to eat your cooking."

He glared at her. "I saw you and Yogurt in that intimate conversation. Is that what you talked about, my cooking? Couldn't you find a more interesting topic?"

"Intimate?" Darryn exclaimed. "What was intimate about it? And we talked about more than your cooking."

"Yeah?" Kirk put his hands on his hips and leaned toward her. "What?"

Darryn stood her ground. "Your love life."

Anger flared in Kirk's eyes, but he controlled it. "Not much more interesting than my cooking, was it?"

"Actually," Darryn said, getting just as angry as Kirk though she couldn't say why, "it was fascinating. I can't wait to hear the rest of the story."

"Well, you won't hear it from me." Kirk stabbed a thumb at his chest. "I guess you'll have to keep working on Yogurt. Just go on baking your *divine* biscuits," his voice dripped sarcasm, "and you'll have him eating out of your hand in a few days. Just like the rest of your court, Princess."

"All I did, oh great leader," Darryn shouted, heedless of who could hear her, "was take my rotation at cooking, just as you demanded. If you didn't want bread, why'd you bring flour? Just to test your swollen masculine ego by carrying it for all these miles?"

She wanted to slap him, but he'd undoubtedly catch her hand and probably hurt her wrist. If she managed to connect with his cheek, all that stubble would hurt her palm. And she'd feel like an idiot. In fact, she felt like an idiot just thinking about it. Heat rushed up her neck into her cheeks, and she hoped Kirk couldn't see it in the dim evening light. She'd probably had a sillier argument sometime, she just couldn't remember when.

"Sorry." She grinned sheepishly. "I didn't mean all that."

"Which parts *did* you mean?" Kirk wasn't exactly grinning but his frown softened. "The part about my swollen ego?"

"Yeah," she laughed. "That part for sure."

Kirk laughed too and once again took her elbow to walk her to her tent. His grip grew more relaxed as they walked. When he finally broke the silence his voice had lost its former hard edge.

"I hate cooking so badly," he said. "With everyone expending so much energy every day, I'd like them to look forward to meals instead of dreading them. A wom...someone who hiked with us a few years ago told me I could double my prices if I'd spend a little time on the food aspect of my business."

"Then why don't you?"

Kirk rolled his eyes. "I know you won't believe this, but I try."

Darryn chewed hard on the inside of her lip to keep from laughing. "I could teach you a few things," she said. "I'm not much good at it either. Who is these days? Everyone works and buys frozen dinners." She shot him a sideways glance to see if his easy mood was still intact. "Why do you care anyway? I mean do you need to double your income?"

"Not exactly."

They reached her tent, and Kirk unzipped the screen and gestured her inside. Darryn wondered if he meant to drop the conversation there, but he crawled in after her and flicked on her lantern. The tent, though small and dimly lit, seemed a sanctuary in the wilderness, with room for just the two of them.

Because she wanted him to stay, Darryn ignored her conscience's warning that their isolation from the others, with walls this time to make their privacy complete, was exactly the situation she'd resolved to avoid.

"Not exactly?" she asked, wanting to keep conversation going in the sudden closeness.

"I don't need much," Kirk said. "If everything went on the same forever, I could live on what I make now for the rest of my life." He sat cross-legged, leaning against his pack. "But things change. I know that."

Darryn sat cross-legged too, but her knees brushed against Kirk's. She pressed back and bumped into her pack. Grabbing her ankles, she curled her legs closer to her body. "What things?" she asked.

"Most things," he said. "The economy, the fees for guiding in the wilderness, my age. I won't be able to do this forever, not at the pace I go now. I'd like to start a climbing school, get it really established, before I have to cut back on these trips."

"That sounds expensive," Darryn said. "Can you save enough just from—"

Kirk's hands resting on his knees clenched into fists. "There're ways to finance it, but I want...intend to cover the cost from my income as a guide." He raised his eyes to hers, not troubling to hide the intensity glowing there.

"Your self-sufficiency means a lot to you."

"Isn't that obvious from what I do?"

"Is that all you want?" Darryn traced her tongue along her bottom lip, trying to ignore the confinement of the tent. "Do you always want...just to know you can make it alone? What if you...I mean, maybe someday you might want to share..." She stopped, sure the heat in her cheeks looked bright red to Kirk.

"Yeah, I might." He laughed softly, all the anger gone from his eyes, replaced by male warmth. "A little more disposable income wouldn't hurt if I ever want to...give up my monklike existence back in civilization.''

Darryn wished Kirk had left the tent flap open. The temperature in the little space had risen noticeably. She felt the heat on her skin, felt it sweeping through her as well. She wondered if Kirk felt it.

"I'll never try to survive there year-round though. Get an inside job, sit at a desk, wear a tie, play the game." Kirk shook his head. "I'll make a living here or I'll starve. And I'll do it myself. I won't be dependent on some...cook to make my trips worth taking."

"Your trips are worth taking now, Kirk." Darryn sat very stiffly, controlling her desire to squeeze Kirk's hand.

"Thanks." Kirk didn't seem to share Darryn's nervousness. He looked completely at ease, one elbow resting behind him on his pack.

Silence fell between them. Night sounds began to filter through the tent: the rustle of trees and the chit-chit-chit of a small nocturnal creature chewing through a pinecone.

Darryn heard them as if at a great distance. Instead she heard the sound of Kirk's breathing, the pounding of her heart in her chest as her own respiration increased from his nearness. She didn't dare look at him to see how he was reacting. She looked down, surprised to see her feet still covered with wet slippers.

"Ugh," she said, tugging them off. "My feet are freezing. I'd better get them inside my sleeping bag."

She hoped he'd take the hint and leave. And she hoped he wouldn't. Darryn forced her gaze to meet his.

"Good idea." The composure in Kirk's posture did not extend to his eyes. They looked silvery hot, intent on Darryn. But he kept the conversation on a safe subject. "I'll just look at your blisters, then hit the sack myself."

"I can do it."

"I said I'll check them."

Something in his tone told her arguing would simply waste her breath. She pulled off her wet socks and tried to put her foot upside down where he could see the back of her heel. She twisted her leg one way, then the other.

With an amused shake of his head, Kirk grabbed her ankles and flipped her onto her stomach. In her yellow cotton hiking shorts, she felt more exposed than last night when her nightie had covered her to her ankles. Though she knew the sensation had more to do with the moments they'd shared after the hike than the expanse of leg she was presenting to Kirk, she wished she could pull the sleeping bag over her.

But Kirk didn't seem to notice. Gently, he removed the bandages he'd applied that morning. "Not great," he said. "But they ought to heal quite a bit tomorrow, since you won't be hiking."

He held each ankle as he dabbed antiseptic all over the back of her right heel, then the left. "Sorry about the sting."

Darryn swallowed. "It's not bad."

Actually she didn't notice it at all. She could hardly believe he was using the same antiseptic. The only burning she felt was on her skin beneath Kirk's callused grip on her ankle. As soon as he'd finished, she rolled over and sat up, drawing her legs tight against her chest.

She had completely lost control of this situation. Every time she was around Kirk, her feelings seemed to intensify. She wanted him to go on holding her leg, or maybe release it and take her in his arms.

She squeezed her arms tighter around her bent knees. "Thanks, Kirk. There's your bivi sac. Sorry you have to sleep outside."

Kirk's smile sent shivers down her spine. He must realize how much he was affecting her. But if he was feeling the same things, he didn't let on.

"No problem," he said, grabbing his gear. "Sleep well."

Darryn changed into her nightie and slipped inside her bag, pulling it up over her head as if she could keep out thoughts of what was happening to her. How could she let her emotions get so out of hand—in only two days? She had nineteen more days to spend alone with Kirk.

She felt like a blushing schoolgirl with a crush on a teacher: a crush she didn't want because there couldn't be a happy ending.

Pushing her fists into her eyes, Darryn forced herself to remember why she'd taken this trip. She pictured Peter Tretherwell, how handsome he'd looked at that party in a light summer suit, pale blue shirt and club tie. That's how Darryn expected men to look. And Peter was a doctor: no one would ever care if he could cook.

More, he was a doctor in her father's practice. All her life, Darryn had wished to somehow remain connected to her father and his work after she left home. When she was very young, she'd often gone on rounds with him and had loved the way the nurses and patients seemed to hold him in awe, just as she did. But she'd only had to take one biology class, to know *she* would never be his partner.

When she'd met Peter at that party and realized he was as attracted to her as she was to him, it was like a dream come true. Though she had only known him a few hours, Darryn had gone to sleep that night, imagining what it would be like to be married to one of Daddy's partners.

Now she was feeling things for Kirk that made those girlish imaginings seem tame. This was more than simple attraction: it was chemical or biological or maybe even psychic. And worse, it was utter madness. Kirk's strength and independence were a large part of what made him so intriguing, but they made the idea of life with him impossible. He wanted to live in the woods in a tent for the rest of his life.

No matter what Darryn felt for him, she would stop this, get it under control. She was not a schoolgirl anymore. The decisions she made now would have a lasting effect on her life. And she knew what kind of a life she wanted, she'd known for years. She couldn't let Kirk...no, herself, blow her dreams now.

Darryn rolled over, determined to sleep soundly till dawn. It was the first of hundreds of times she rolled over that night, aching for her thoughts to leave her alone and let her sleep. Not one of those thoughts was ever about Peter Tretherwell.

At dawn, though she had barely slept, Darryn was relieved to hear sounds of human movement outside her tent. She could hardly wait to leave her self-imposed prison cell. She groped around for her slippers, couldn't find them, and crawled to the opening barefoot.

Kirk had hung her slippers from one of the tent ribs in the vestibule. The fuzzy pink fur, though a little stiff, had dried thoroughly in the night. Darryn was touched that he'd thought of it. Putting them on, she crawled outside, saw Kirk over by the cook stove, and headed into the trees.

When she returned, Kirk handed her a cup of coffee and, motioning her for quiet, walked a distance with her away from the tents. Whey they could see the lake, he sat on a large boulder and patted the sun warmed rock beside him.

"You don't look like you slept too well, Princess," he said as she sat. "What are you doing up so early?"

"I, uh..." She sipped her coffee, unwilling to tell him she'd spent the night tossing and turning, thinking about him. "Actually I slept like a log."

Kirk raised his brows. "Yeah, right." He touched the skin beneath her eyes. "Do you always put purple eye shadow under here?"

"You convinced me," Darryn explained, "dawn is the most beautiful time of day. Too beautiful to miss. I guess really," she pointed at the reflection of sunrise on the glasslike surface of the lake, "that convinced me. I'm sorry I let Jordan talk me out of carrying along my sketchbook.''

''I am too,'' Kirk said. ''It'd be worth a little extra weight to see some of your drawings—the way you notice things. Too bad you can't see it in the winter, that's the most beautiful time.''

Darryn shuddered. ''You come here in the winter?''

''I've never come right here,'' Kirk said. ''But we do winter climbs. Nothing more beautiful than a frozen waterfall in the sunshine with all the world around it white and soft. Snow takes the hard edges off everything.''

''I think I'll skip it,'' Darryn said. ''Isn't it much more dangerous than climbing in the summer?''

''Yeah, the weather's worse. Weather's usually what kills climbers, any time of year.''

Darryn looked back at the face he meant to climb today. ''Why do you do it?''

''I love it, Darryn. The first time I got to the top of a face and looked down and saw what I'd done, I...'' Kirk frowned as if seeking the right word. ''I was hooked, I guess. I used to try to explain it to people, to get them interested in it. Now I just do it.''

''I'm afraid of heights,'' Darryn said.

''So am I.''

Darryn gawked at him.

Smiling broadly, Kirk touched the skin under her chin and pushed her gaping mouth shut. ''Everyone is. That's what makes it a challenge.''

''I think I'll just go for a little hike, so I don't have to watch you.''

Kirk's easy mood dissipated. ''Not alone, Darryn. Three of you don't want to climb. If you hike, go with Tim, he's done this a lot. Or all of you go together.''

''I won't go far,'' she insisted. ''I just want a little solitude.''

Kirk shook his head vehemently. ''I told you the first day, forget privacy. No one goes off alone. Understand?''

Darryn glared at him, unwilling to explain that she needed time alone to sort out her thoughts about him.

Staring fixedly at her lower lip, Kirk grinned broadly. "I see by your pout that you understand perfectly."

Darryn didn't bother to deny that she ever pouted, but she pulled in her lip, changing her expression to a glower. "I guess I'll go start breakfast."

"Good idea," Kirk said. "Since it's my turn to cook, I'm sure everyone will be grateful you got up early."

She gave him a final frown and headed toward the cooking area.

"Don't take it so hard, Princess," Kirk said to her back. "It's not really harder to do as you're told than to hike twelve miles at high altitude. It just feels like it because it's your first time."

Kirk laughed heartily at his rotten joke, but Darryn did not deign to respond.

CHAPTER SIX

DARRYN had been wrong about a lot of things on this trip, but her decision not to watch Kirk, or any of the other men, climb the mountain was not one of them. No matter how her boots felt, she could hardly wait to get out of camp.

She had learned more from the climbers at breakfast than she wanted to know. They didn't even look normal anymore. The last two days, the men had worn rugged hiking clothes. Today they looked like ballet dancers, in skin-hugging Lycra tights that clung to their legs and buttocks, revealing every smallest muscle movement.

Since Kirk spent all his time engaged in physical pursuits, it wasn't fair to compare him to the other men who only got to do this sort of thing once a year. But Darryn couldn't help it. Her gaze returned again and again to his sinewy masculine form. Fortunately, none of the others seemed to notice her lingering stares at Kirk. They were all too interested in his talk about the climb to pay attention to anything else.

"There're several ways to go," Kirk had explained, "but the one I'd like to try looks like it has at least one five-ten pitch, maybe five-eleven. Anyone interested?"

Darryn had no idea what he was talking about, but it wasn't hard to figure out that a five-ten was hard and a five-eleven harder. Three of the men, the ones who looked in the best shape, acted very interested. She tried to ignore the proceedings after that but couldn't. The more advanced climbers, they decided, would follow Kirk up a difficult route, while the other two would follow Yogurt up a five-eight. Since Kirk would be taking three with him, they would need to use a more complex system of ropes.

73

Darryn's nervousness grew more apparent during this discussion, until Alex made the ridiculous statement, "Don't worry, Darryn, we won't take any chances."

"How can you say that?" she asked. "Look where you're going."

"It's much safer than it looks," he said, "with the harnesses and all the protection. Kirk's a very careful leader. He never places bad pro."

"Bad pro?"

Alex turned to Kirk. "Did you show her your rack?"

When Kirk shook his head, Alex went to get it. A few minutes later he returned with a loop of something that looked like rolled canvas from which hung dozens of metal devices.

"See?" Alex said. "We have all these to hold us to the mountain."

Darryn looked at them suspiciously. "You hammer those things into the rock?"

"No," Kirk said adamantly. "You're thinking of pitons. No one uses them anymore, they destroy the rock for anyone coming after. The leader puts these cams and stoppers in cracks, then hooks the rope to them. The climber following takes them out. That way, we leave nothing behind. No marks of where we've climbed."

Darryn lifted one of the stoppers, a small piece of metal less than a third of an inch square, with a wire loop attached. "You put this tiny little thing in a crack and hang your lives from it?"

"It can hold hundreds of pounds, Darryn," Will assured her. "If the lead climber takes a fall, he won't fall more than twice the distance from his last protection. The followers can't fall more than a few inches, really."

"Right." Darryn stared at the rack of protection devices. Several were larger than the one she'd picked out and shaped differently. But none had more than a small wire attachment to hold a rope, the climbers' lifeline. "Those things never come out?"

No one seemed to want to answer that.

"Occasionally, little one," Yogurt finally said. "But we are very careful, Kirk and I. Kirk has not fallen on one of these trips for years."

She met his sparkling black eyes. "You and Kirk are the leaders, of course."

"Of course." For once Yogurt did not smile. "These men are our friends but also our clients. We do not let them lead, no matter what they wish."

Darryn looked at the mountain. In some places the rock looked not just steep but overhanging. How could anyone hold on to it there? "Have you ever climbed here before?"

"No," Kirk said, excitement in his voice. "I want to on-sight my route."

She stared. "On-sight? How else would you climb it? With your eyes closed?"

When the laughter died down, Kirk said, "On-sight means to climb a new route without a fall."

As Kirk began to describe the two routes to the others, Darryn went to her tent to get ready for her hike.

Roger joined her a few minutes later. "Where to?" he said, pulling on his pack.

"I thought we might hike, well stroll, down to that lake," Darryn said. "Saunter, maybe. Nothing like Kirk's pace yesterday."

The weight of Kirk's fanny pack filled with water bottles and trail mix pulled at her waist as she clipped it around her middle.

"That lake is a lot farther away than you think," said Roger. "Kirk said we ought to take it easy on your blistered feet."

"How nice he's worried about me," she said, her lips thining in irritation at his officiousness. "Where's Tim?"

"He's staying here," Roger said. "Wants a day off."

"I know how he feels."

Roger regarded her curiously. "Why don't you stay too?" he asked. "Relax and read a book."

"I didn't bring a book."

"I could lend you one. I always bring two."

"A mystery?"

Roger shook his head. "A history of the Indian wars and a book on quantum mechanics."

Darryn rolled her eyes. "Let's hike. You lead since you think the lake is too far away. I don't care where we go."

Three hours later, Roger brought them back to camp after a hike that had filled Darryn with satisfaction. Though they had walked nearly twice as long as she'd planned, never once had she wanted to quit or even lie down and complain. She could hardly wait to drag her aching feet out of her boots, but her legs and lungs felt strong.

Despite her fierce admonition to herself to keep her eyes on the ground, Darryn found herself at the base of the climb with her gaze riveted on the climbers. They looked like spiders, webbed to the cliff with rope, clinging precariously to invisible cracks in the rock.

"Strange," said Roger.

"What's strange?" Darryn gripped his wrist. "Do you see something wrong? Are they in danger?"

"Take it easy, Darryn," he assured her. "There's nothing wrong. I'm just surprised to see Yogurt that much higher up the face than Kirk. Kirk climbs faster than Yogurt, and he's leading more experienced climbers." He shaded his eyes with his hand. "Hey, Kirk," he shouted, "having some trouble on that pitch?"

"She's back, Kirk," Darryn heard Alex yell. "Think you can stay on the rock now?"

"*Dieu merci*, Kirk!" Yogurt shouted. "Perhaps you will survive the climb after all."

Roars of laughter from men on both routes echoed down the mountain. Kirk shouted vulgarities, but he laughed too. Obviously teasing about his climbing skills didn't disturb his serenity an iota.

Kirk must have shaken off whatever had slowed him while she and Roger were gone, for he now moved rapidly up the cliff with no hesitation. Yogurt moved with more starts and stops—and swearing. In fact, all the climbers swore loudly and often, constantly accusing each other of whining.

Darryn told herself repeatedly to go to her tent, but she couldn't pull her gaze away. In fact, she quit blinking, afraid that if she looked away for a second something dreadful would happen. She had no idea how long she stood rigidly tense, staring up, till Roger returned.

"You still here?" he asked. "I've had a nap and you haven't moved."

"A nap?" Darryn tried to relax her taut muscles. "How can you sleep when—?"

"I used to climb with Kirk every summer," Roger said. "I know how safe they are."

"Why'd you quit?"

"I broke my heel, shattered it actually into about a hundred pieces." He made a self-deprecating noise. "I'm lucky I can still hike with him."

"I'm surprised he lets you," Darryn said.

"I had to twist his arm damned hard," Roger admitted. "He only agreed after he heard I finished a ten K race."

"That sounds like Kirk." Darryn looked skyward and her heart fluttered. "Oh Lord, what's he doing now?"

"It's an overhang," Roger said. "With a roof to come. Pretty brutal."

Kirk hung nearly upside down from a jutting point of rock that anyone with sense, Darryn thought, would have climbed around. Looking like a human fly, he crawled slowly along it, never taking more than one extremity off the rock at a time. From where Darryn stood, it looked like Kirk held himself to the rock as much with his feet as his fingers.

"Can the others do that?"

"I doubt it," Roger said. "But Kirk'll have them top-roped. And they have ascenders."

"What's that?"

"A device that lets them climb the rope instead of the rock."

"Does Kirk have one?"

"No, but he can climb the rock. Watch his moves."

"I *am* watching!" Darryn exclaimed. "It's terrifying."

From the corner of her eye, Darryn saw Roger's frown. He didn't look angry, just curious. Darryn felt heat steal into her cheeks. She sounded like Kirk's wife or his girl-friend, instead of just his client. Her too vocal anxiety revealed far too much emotion to Roger—or perhaps to herself. But she didn't have the time or composure right now to figure out why Kirk's position up there frightened her so much.

"Maybe you should read in your tent," Roger said. "I brought you the history book."

"I don't think history could get my attention just now," Darryn said, her jaw clenched tight. "Is that the roof? How can he ever get over it?"

"Didn't you hear him describe it this morning?"

"I tried not to pay attention."

Roger nodded as if he understood. "See how he's got his hands backwards now? That's an undercling."

Darryn looked, swallowing despite the dryness in her throat. Kirk had lodged himself under a shelf of rock that stuck straight out over him at least two feet beyond his head. His feet pressed against the wall of rock, pushing him out as he clung backwards to a crack in the corner.

"He's got to reach out to the edge of the roof with one hand," Roger explained. "But when he does, his feet won't have any opposing resistance to press against, and they'll come off the wall."

"Good heavens," Darryn breathed.

"Watch me here!" they heard Kirk shout. "It's really thin."

"I've got you," Alex hollered.

Darryn clenched and unclenched her teeth a dozen times as Kirk suddenly lunged for the edge and grabbed it with his right hand. His feet swung free, waving precariously, while he maneuvered his left hand onto the ledge. When he finally hung from both hands, he began walking a foot up the underside of the roof to the ledge by his hands.

"Heel jam," Roger muttered.

Without a jerk or a stop, Kirk hauled himself smoothly over the edge of the roof.

"Oohh," she sighed, all her muscles sagging from the release of tension.

Kirk tied himself to the ledge he'd reached. "Off belay," he shouted.

Darryn rubbed the back of her neck, which ached from staring up for so long. No matter how insane the whole thing looked to her, she couldn't miss the exhilaration in Kirk's voice at having climbed the overhang without a fall. She transferred her gaze to Yogurt and was startled to find him a full rope length lower than Kirk now.

She looked at Roger. "Wow, he is fast, isn't he?"

Roger nodded. "He's smooth too. From here you can't see at all how hard he's working. I bet he's soaking with sweat right now, but he made it look easy, didn't he?"

"Not to me," Darryn said, but something in Roger's tone bothered her. "You really miss it, don't you?"

"You'd have to try it to understand how much."

"Then I won't ever understand." She turned back to the climbers. "When will they come down?"

Roger looked up, mentally calculating. "Probably one more pitch."

"I think I will take a nap," Darryn said, trying to sound casual.

She was sure she'd never sleep a wink, but she needed to get away from here to get a rein on her emotions. She couldn't stand around with Roger, gasping every time Kirk made a move. He'd think she had special feelings for Kirk, which of course wasn't true. She was worried about all the men on the mountain. She'd just watched Kirk because his route had been so much more...intense.

Darryn had just reached her tent when she heard Alex shout, "Climbing!"

Immediately she tilted her stiff neck back to watch him. The pitch seemed to take forever. None of the other men on Kirk's rope could climb the overhang, but each of them had to try it several times before giving up. By the time the last man had reached Kirk's ledge, Yogurt's team had again caught up. By then Kirk was leading the next pitch, and Darryn's feet had unconsciously brought her back to the base of the climb.

Before all the men had climbed the last pitch, Darryn was sure a geological epoch had passed. Another age elapsed while they fiddled around at the top with ropes and harnesses and knots and who knew what all.

Finally Kirk hollered, "On rappel." Stepping to the edge, he turned his back and fell off the top.

Darryn screamed and lurched toward the cliff.

Roger grabbed her from behind. "He's okay, Darryn."

"He fell."

"No, he's rapelling. It's the easiest way down."

With her hands covering her face, Darryn shook all over, even her heart trembled. Terror, relief and shame swept through her, bringing burning tears to her eyes. "I thought... It looked like he fell."

"He's fine. Look."

Darryn looked up. Kirk stood straight out from the rock as he walked and jumped backwards down the side of the mountain. From his whoops and shouts, he was obviously enjoying himself. He certainly wasn't falling. Yet it appeared more dangerous than anything Darryn had seen him do so far.

Feeling foolish but still frightened, she shrugged Roger's hands off her shoulders. Kirk's movements looked careless...well, at least carefree. Yet he was still hundreds of feet above the ground. The risk hadn't passed, but these men were behaving as if it had.

Darryn couldn't watch anymore. She fled.

In the blue tinted solitude of her tent, Darryn crumpled onto her sleeping bag and leaned her head in her hands. Of all the emotions sweeping through her, fear reigned uppermost. The thought of Kirk's body lying crushed and bleeding on the rocks after a six hundred foot fall still had her insides quaking.

But behind the fear came a swirl of other emotions about Kirk—attraction, frustration, affection, desire, anger, passion, curiosity, admiration—that left her bewildered and upset. All the things she felt about Kirk seemed too intense, too conflicting, for such a brief acquaintance. The immensity of the wilderness, their isolation, the life-threatening nature of Kirk's sport, must make all her feelings sharper than they'd be at . . . well, certainly at a cocktail party.

Darryn sat up and began tugging at her bootlaces. No wonder her feet throbbed, she'd worn these darn stiff boots for hours. Thinking about anything besides her confusion and fear soothed her, and she gave the boots her undivided attention. Luckily, she'd gotten a nasty knot in one lace, which she'd even managed somehow to get wet. Untying it took long minutes.

"Darryn, are you decent?" Kirk's voice came through the nylon. "I need to use the tent."

He sounded stilted. Darryn wondered if Roger had told him about her panic at the base of the rock. She dragged the second boot off her foot, donned her slippers and crawled outside. "Go on in, it's all your—"

Darryn's words stuck in her throat. Still on all fours, she stared at the gruesome sight of Kirk's knees. "Oh my heavens," she said, swallowing hard.

The stretch fabric of his climbing tights had torn and shredded over both knees. The flesh beneath looked in much the same shape as the tattered cloth. Blood oozed from cuts and scratches, and the left kneecap had a deep wide cut across it. Both knees were black and blue where they weren't raspberry red, and the left looked too swollen to bend comfortably.

"Kirk," she stood up, glad to raise her eyes from the level of his injuries. "What happened?"

"Just a scrape," he said. "Mind if I use the tent to clean up?"

She pointed at his left leg. "That one needs stitches."

Kirk stepped back. "Butterfly bandages will do the trick."

"Hardly. Maybe you could—"

"Darryn," Kirk said, pushing both palms toward her, "don't even think about it. Your father's the doctor, not you. Where the hell did you go for so long anyway?"

"I went for a hike. How did you—"

"I told you to go with Tim."

"You're just trying to change the subject," Darryn said, letting her gaze flick briefly to his knees. "I didn't go alone, I went with Roger."

"Roger!" Kirk said. "With his bad foot? You never know how far that foot will take him. What the hell would you have—?"

"How did I know he had a bad foot?" Darryn said. "Besides, what could happen? If he'd collapsed, I could have come for help. Isn't that the point of taking two?"

"What could happen?" Kirk echoed, rubbing his fingers hard across his brow. "Do you know how Roger crushed his foot? Taking dumb chances, that's how."

"Well, I didn't know that and nothing happened, so quit yelling at me." Darryn put her hands on her hips and glared at him. She realized her irritation with this silly conversation had dispelled most of her fear. That realization, however, let her feel how glad she was to see Kirk. "Besides you're the one who got injured. How did you hurt your knees?" Her voice came out softer, but she couldn't help it.

"A momentary lapse of concentration," Kirk said. "That's all it takes." He frowned at her as if considering whether to elaborate, then fell silent.

"Tell me the rest, Kirk."

He shrugged. "I saw Tim below us. Yogurt hollered down to him, asking where you guys had hiked. When he said you'd gone alone with Roger, a lot of bad memories of Roger's accident came back to me, and I...peeled off the rock."

"Are you trying to blame me for this mess on your knees?"

"Not at all," Kirk said. "But I'm responsible for everyone on this trip. If you don't believe me, talk to my insurance company. You signed an agreement to follow the safety rules when you registered for the trip."

"I followed the rules, I didn't go alone. You're worrying about nothing."

"No, Princess." Kirk cupped her chin in his hand, his fingers still gritty from the chalk he used climbing. "I'm worrying about you. It's a damned helpless feeling to be halfway through an eight hour climb and hear you're off somewhere unknown, too long, with someone who may not be watching out for you properly."

"Watching out for me? I'm all grown up, Kirk. I can watch out for myself." She poked him in the chest and he grimaced in pain. "Oh no. Did you hurt your chest, too?"

He nodded, taking shallow breaths and pressing his forearm against his chest. "The rock was out-sloping where I fell. I had to push off to keep from crashing down it. The rope caught me at a funny angle at the end of its arc and pulled the muscles around my ribs a little. That's how it jerked my knees into my face. I'll be fine by tomorrow."

Darryn eyed him anxiously. "What makes you say that? You look awful."

Kirk grinned mockingly. "Thanks, Princess. Don't worry, I'll put ice on everything, and it won't even slow me down tomorrow."

"What if you'd been killed?"

"Killed?" Kirk exclaimed. "From a fifteen foot fall? No way. I told you, I don't take chances. You took a bigger risk hiking with Roger."

Darryn remembered her terror when she thought Kirk had fallen, and she couldn't answer. She spun away to keep him from seeing the concern on her face. Kirk grabbed her arm and pulled her back to him.

"Darryn?" He took her head between his hands and tilted up her face. "Were you really scared?"

She closed her eyes, nodding. "When you came down, over the top, it looked like you fell. I'd gotten so tense watching you all that time. Then you just dropped that way..."

"I heard something, a scream I thought. Was that you?"

"Mm hmm. You looked...even after I knew you weren't falling, you looked...careless. But you were still so far up. The danger wasn't over."

He pulled her against his chest carefully and stroked her short hair. "You're dead right. Rappelling is dangerous just because of that. All your adrenaline is gone, everything you used for the climb. You think it's over and relax and don't pay enough attention. There're more accidents rapping than climbing." He nudged her under the chin, and she looked at him. "But, I repeat, I don't take chances. I don't relax when I rap, no matter how it looks."

"You just admitted you sometimes lose your concentration."

He gave her a considering look. "Next time, you ought to try it."

"No!" she cried. "You can't be serious. Never. I'd panic."

"I doubt it. And I wouldn't take you up something like we climbed today. Just a simple pitch. Just so you could feel how safe it is, with the ropes and harness and shoes."

"Kirk, I just spent hours wondering if you were going to die." Darryn's fear returned despite her efforts to control it and her voice shook. "We'd be lost here without you."

"No, you wouldn't. That's why Yogurt and I work together. He could lead you out."

"I like Yogurt." Darryn pushed away from Kirk, carefully so as not to hurt his ribs or brush his knees. She couldn't think clearly with him holding her. "But I don't want to put my life in his hands. I don't trust him the way I trust you."

Kirk grinned broadly. "That's a helluva compliment, coming from the woman who thought I meant to kill her the first day out."

"I guess that's funny," Darryn said, not laughing. "But I never felt unsafe with you until today. And I don't want to get any closer to the experience than I already have." She fluttered a hand through the air as if she could throw away her fear. "Next time I don't even want to watch you. I wish I didn't have to know you were up a face. How many days are you going to climb?"

Kirk's grin faded. "Five more days. That's a lot of days to condemn yourself to terror, Darryn. Terror that could be alleviated by learning a few techniques. Even if you don't like it, I promise you, you won't be terrified anymore." He took one of her hands and stroked soothingly over the palm with the pad of his thumb. "You just said you trusted me."

"I trust you," Darryn said. "I just don't want to watch you climb. Think about you falling, smashing on the rocks."

"Me?" Kirk asked, his voice deep. "Or all of us?"

Heat flooded Darryn's cheeks. "Oh... I mean... of course, all of you. I just meant... well, you were out in front." She kept her eyes downcast, watching his thumb moving over her palm till no tension remained in her anywhere.

"I have to agree with you." She could hear laughter back in his voice. "I'd hate to see me smash on the rocks too. But I have no intention of coming even close."

"Just like you had no intention of smashing your knees today?"

Kirk sighed. "I guess I can't convince you. But thanks for worrying about me, it's kind of nice actually."

She snapped her gaze up, meaning to rebuke him for sarcasm, but his smile looked genuine and warm. Too warm. She pulled her hand free. "You'd better do something about your knees or you won't be able to walk."

"Too true," he said. "Want to help?"

"Ugh, no!" Darryn said. "I can't handle stuff like that. At all. If I could bandage cuts like that, I wouldn't be up here in the first place."

Kirk cocked his head. "What do you mean?"

"I'd be in medical school, becoming a cardiologist like Daddy so I could go into practice with him."

"Cardiologists never hike?" Kirk sounded confused.

"No, I just wouldn't have...agreed..." Darryn paused, regretting she'd brought the subject up. "It was a doctor..." She hesitated again then spoke in a rush. "I'm here because I promised the new doctor I'd show him all about mountains and backpacking when he moves to Billings."

A frown was slowly settling onto Kirk's face. "And if you were a doctor yourself you wouldn't have done that?"

"I doubt it."

"Because you wouldn't be so damn impressed by doctors if you were one yourself."

"That's not it at all," Darryn said. "I'm not impressed by all doctors. I know how bad some of them are."

"Just by 'Daddy' and his pals."

"You're darn right, Daddy!" she exclaimed. "He's a brilliant surgeon. Ask anyone. Ask some of the people whose lives he's saved. I admire him as much as I love him. What's wrong with that? Don't you love your father?"

Kirk's eyes narrowed. "I love my father enough. But I sure as hell never let him tell me who to date based on some criterion of wealth or social standing."

"Daddy doesn't tell me who I can date."

"Yeah?" Kirk put his hands on his hips. "What would he say if you showed up with some scruffy guy in the wrong tax bracket?"

"I have no idea," Darryn said. "Because I've never done that before. But I'm sure he'd be open-minded."

"Right." Kirk shook his head. "Go ahead and kid yourself if you want, Darryn. But it seems pretty dumb to throw yourself at a man you hardly know simply because he happens to work with Daddy."

"Throw myself?" Darryn's voice quivered with rage at the insult but she couldn't bring herself to deny it outright for she had an uncomfortable feeling it was at least partly true. "How dare you say such a thing? How I act in the civilized world is none of your business. Besides, you weren't there."

"I didn't need to be." His tone reminded her of their conversations the first day. The rapport she'd worked so hard to build with Kirk had vanished. "Believe me, Princess, I can picture the whole scene exactly."

Kirk took two stiff steps to the tent, sat down and crawled in backwards to avoid scraping his knees. Darryn stared at the tent screen waving in the breeze. She wanted to yell something at him, something that would make him change his mind about her, take that remote ex-

pression off his face. But she could think of nothing
convincing—nothing honest and convincing anyway.

Kirk hadn't really said anything she could deny. Certainly she idolized her father, he was a wonderful man.
Of course she wished she could find someone like him.
Who wouldn't? But it was also true, heaven knows, that
she wouldn't have agreed to take Peter Tretherwell
camping in September if she'd had to return to medical
school herself. Worse, she had to wonder—in fact she'd
wondered since the champagne wore off—if she had
exaggerated Peter's attractiveness in her own mind just
because he was going to be Daddy's partner.

But why had it all made Kirk so angry? Especially
after the last two days when she thought they had put
aside their differences and were becoming friends.
Darryn thought over Kirk's wrathful words. Despite his
displeasure over her hiking alone, he hadn't gotten really
upset with her till he heard about Peter.

Could Kirk be jealous? Jealous of Darryn and another
man?

Kirk?

She stared at the tent as if she could find an answer
there. She saw only yellow and blue nylon, heard Kirk's
grunted oaths as he did something painful to his knees.
He didn't sound one bit like a jealous man pining over
his woman.

No, he might envy someone who could climb an
overhang he couldn't. But she doubted Kirk Storm, with
all his self-confidence, had ever suffered a moment's
jealousy over anything as commonplace as a woman.

CHAPTER SEVEN

DARRYN awoke next morning to rustling sounds in her tent. Slitting open one eye, she discovered Kirk, sitting cross-legged with his back to her, packing both their packs. He'd barely said a civil word to her last night. She wondered if he was still in a snit.

"Kirk?"

He jumped, then grunted, pressing his wrist to his ribs. "Finally awake, Princess?" he said. "Good. You need to pack up the sleeping bags."

Darryn gave him a long considering look. She wished she could raise one brow, the way he did. "If you think you can carry all my things when your ribs hurt that way, you're nuts, Kirk. Put some stuff in my pack."

Kirk shook his head dismissively. "No way. I'm not weaker than I was yesterday, I just ache a little. You're not strong enough to carry more." He stuffed a black leather case into the bottom of one of the side pouches on his pack. "I'll loosen up after a few minutes on the trail."

"What's that leather thing?" Darryn asked, wondering how to avoid, or at least win, the argument she could see coming.

"The radio," Kirk said.

"What do you listen to, country and western?"

Kirk flashed a mirthless grin. "It's for emergencies, in case we need a helicopter rescue." He picked up something silver and bullet shaped, the size of a rolled magazine. "And this is the water purifier." He stuffed it in his pack and turned to her. "Want to see the ditty bag of your clothes and things you're leaving behind?"

"No," Darryn said. "I don't even want to think about those things till we get back to them." She paused. "But

89

I want you to put the radio and a climbing rope in my pack. They're both heavy enough to make you wince.''

"No can do, Princess," he said. "We're going to hike fourteen miles today. You'd never make it."

Darryn pulled herself partly out of her bag and leaned up on her elbows. "If you don't put some weight in my pack, Kirk, *you* won't make it fourteen miles either."

He didn't look up from his packing job. "Of course I will."

"No, you won't. I'll see to it."

He stopped, a jar of jelly in his hand, to stare at her. "How will you manage that?"

"I'll take too long getting ready, I'll fall asleep after lunch. I'll sprain my ankle and slow everyone down. I won't eat or drink and I'll collapse again. And if anyone asks me why, I'll tell them what a stubborn foolish egomaniac you're being."

During this speech, Kirk's expression changed from mocking grin to genuine smile. "You're used to getting your own way, aren't you, Brat?" Keeping a wrist pressed to his side, he pulled in a deep breath and let it out slowly as if testing his ribs. "But I guess I could use the help."

"Good thinking, Kirk."

He looked at the stuff still scattered on the floor of the tent. "I'll give you the radio and the purifier. Maybe the stove. The rope's too heavy and awkward." He reached across the small space that separated them and squeezed her hand. "Thanks, Darryn. If you change your mind any time during the day, let me know."

Darryn nodded. The tent seemed to shrink when Kirk touched her, as if his gentle grip was pulling her closer. With sleep still fogging her brain, she couldn't remember why that was a bad idea. Then he released her and turned back to his packing.

Darryn stretched and yawned, trying to feel as nonchalant as he acted. "Kirk, if you had a radio all along, why didn't you send me home the first day?"

"Yeah, right." He chuckled. "I can hear it now. 'We've got a spoiled brat up here who's changed her mind and wants a ride home. Mind sending a heli-taxi?'" He shook his head. "Wouldn't do much for our credibility and it'd cost you a fortune."

Darryn couldn't think of a response. She slithered the rest of the way out of her sleeping bag and rose to her knees, looking for the small bag of toiletries Kirk let her keep. A sigh escaped him, and she glanced his way to see if he'd hurt his ribs again. He looked anything but in pain.

Kirk's eyes traced up and down her kneeling form. "I was going to put that ridiculous nightgown in the bag of stuff to leave behind." He shook his head, his gaze never leaving her scantily covered figure. "But I can't. Thinking of you wearing it every night is becoming my favorite part of this trip."

Darryn brought her searching gaze back to Kirk's, remembering too late what showed through her nightie. More than his words, Kirk's smoldering look and husky tone informed her that his keen eyesight had not missed a thing.

She struggled against the answering warmth sweeping through her and forced herself to keep the situation light. "Don't even consider it, Kirk Storm. If my nightie isn't in my pack tonight, you'll be hiking back here to get it for me." She pulled her fuzzy slippers on her feet. "These too."

Kirk regarded the slippers with resignation. "Those are medicinal, I hate to admit. Your blisters would never heal if you couldn't wear them around camp. Now you'd better hit the trees before all the others get up."

Three mornings later, Darryn crawled outside the tent to enjoy another dawn with Kirk. The last three hikes had been harder than Darryn had expected. She'd crawled into her sleeping bag each night exhausted, barely aware of their wild and beautiful surroundings, too tired to sketch even if she'd had the tools.

But each morning she'd awakened feeling stronger. Each day she'd insisted on carrying more in her pack. Though the weight she bore didn't approach Kirk's, it was coming closer to the other men's.

Her growing strength gave her intense satisfaction and, more important, a sense of independence she'd never had before. Darryn had always thought of independence as getting her own apartment and paying her own rent—unless she ran short and had to call Daddy for a loan.

The independence she felt now was entirely different. It dwarfed having her own apartment. Every day she felt more secure with herself, more confident that she could survive alone, with or without Daddy's backing.

Just as she wished that by the end of the trip, her pack could weigh as much as Kirk's. She liked hiking beside him, following his lead on the trail. But she liked even more the feeling that she could get there on her own.

Not that she wanted "getting there on her own" to mean getting there alone. Of all the feelings that had burgeoned in her the last few days, that one scared her the most: the feeling that she wanted to hike beside Kirk for a lot longer than three weeks.

That one feeling shattered the tranquility her newfound strength and independence had given her, and left her instead with a confusing set of unanswered questions. Like, did she remember why she'd come on this trip in the first place? Or had she changed her mind and decided she wanted something else? Something else from the trip or something else from life? Surely she hadn't changed her mind about *that*, had she?

And what did Kirk feel? She thought he was responding to her too, but she wasn't sure how much. He hadn't made an overt pass since their kiss the second night. But he made sure they hiked together every day.

Two nights ago, desperate for sleep, Darryn had decided how to handle these questions: she was ignoring them and meant to go on doing so. And while she was ignoring them, she planned to spend all the time she could with Kirk. Which certainly included sharing every dawn with him.

When she spotted Kirk in climbing tights, Darryn remembered with a jolt that he meant to climb today. Out of consideration for her, Kirk had made camp last night half a mile away from the climb so Darryn couldn't see the wall. The field of boulders and tufty wind-whipped grass was surrounded by forest.

However, at this altitude the forest was made up not of towering evergreens but scrub pines. Nothing grew taller than about six feet, and most plant life was a good deal shorter than that, a few inches at most. Thus, without much tilt to her neck, Darryn could easily see the mountain they meant to climb today.

It rose above the trees, a vast craggy peak of rock and snow and glacier. This morning the summit was hidden in a cloud, which Darryn anxiously assumed was depositing more snow on the very route Kirk meant to take.

Kirk pulled her away from the tents and stuck a mug of coffee in her hand. "Don't panic, Princess," he said. "I've done this one before."

"It's snowing up there."

"Maybe," he agreed. "We may not make it. That's part of the fun, remember? It's real mountaineering we're doing today, not just rock climbing. This is what it's all about, for me."

"What if it gets late and dark and you—?"

"We'll take bivi sacs and food. We'll have plenty of stuff to spend the night on the mountain."

"On the face?"

Kirk shrugged. "I hope not. But it won't be the first time. Ask Yogurt. He cursed me all night once while we tried to keep warm, roped in a thousand feet up on a three inch ledge. He reminds me of it every time I get too cocky about my climbing."

"You two are crazy."

"Certifiable." Kirk reached inside a pocket in his dark green anorak. "I've got a present for you. Actually I got it a couple of days ago, but you've been too tired at night to use it." He handed her a small spiral notebook and a pencil. "Can you draw in something that small?"

Darryn's eyes lit up and she grabbed the sketching tools. "I can draw in anything. Oh, Kirk, where did you get it?"

"It's Roger's. He keeps a diary." Kirk sat down in the blowing grasses. "But he agreed your need was greater than his. Think it'll take your mind off us crashing down today?"

"Oh yes. More or less. Not exactly." Darryn sat down beside him, facing him, so the sun would warm her back. "I'll still watch, because I want to draw you guys on the mountain, as long as I can see you. But at least it'll make me think about what I'm looking at instead of where you might land if you fall."

"You sound more cheerful about our demise already," Kirk laughed, leaning back on his elbows. "How're the feet?"

"They throb."

"You've carried too much weight. A day off them will help." His gaze flicked toward her slippers. "I'd better cut back on how much goes in your pack."

"Oh honestly, Kirk. You talk like I'm helpless. I feel fine. After all, do I check your ribs every day?"

Kirk gave her a broad grin. "Help yourself," he said. "Want me to take off my shirt?"

"I want you to button your lip. I just haven't softened my boots up all the way, that's all. Don't you dare take anything out of my pack. In fact, I plan to put this sketchbook in there too."

Kirk sat up straight. "Let's see how they look. I need to bandage your blisters before the climb anyway."

"Don't you think I can apply a Band-Aid on my own, Kirk?" She curled her feet away from him.

"You sound like a little kid at a doctor." Kirk leaned over, grabbed her right ankle and lifted her foot into his lap. "Had you ever worn your boots before this trip?"

"No," Darryn said, trying futilely to pull her foot from his grasp.

He removed her slipper and began to rub her foot.

"Kirk, I don't—"

His fingers moved along her arch, tugged at each toe, pressed soothingly against all the sore and swollen places that had borne her weight for so many unfamiliar miles.

Darryn closed her eyes, reveling in the sensations Kirk was creating in her body. Though his strong hands never touched her above the ankle, all her muscles responded, relaxing and melting till she thought she'd dissolve into the earth.

"Don't what, Princess?" Kirk asked, pulling her left foot into his lap to massage it as he had the other.

"I started to say I didn't need this." Darryn put her hands behind her and leaned back. "But I see now that it's an absolute essential. I don't know how I've lived so long without it."

Kirk laughed. "You never needed it this much in your other life. It just pushes the excess fluid out of your tissues," he said. "It'll make it easier to get your boots on today. Your blisters don't look so hot though, a day off will do them good."

Darryn swallowed a sigh of pleasure as all the aches seemed to flow out of her foot and leg. "Kirk, I don't care what it does. Just keep doing it."

Kirk muttered something affirmative and continued his ministrations. When he lowered her foot to the ground, Darryn remained leaning back with her eyes closed. "Maybe I'll go back to bed," she murmured.

"Wouldn't hurt," Kirk said, his voice rough.

Darryn realized the prolonged contact had stirred him too. She sat up but didn't meet his eyes. Her cheeks felt flushed, though she didn't think she was blushing. "Shouldn't the climbers get up soon?" she asked.

Kirk nodded. "Soon enough."

Darryn glanced around. "Maybe we should go for a short hike?"

One side of Kirk's lips curled up into a sardonic grin. "So we can be alone in the woods instead of alone here at camp?"

Darryn shook her head, then nodded. "At least we'd be moving."

She sat up straight to put on her slippers and looked toward the forest. If they hiked, in a few steps trees would surround them, hiding them from camp.

"On second thought, maybe I'll start breakfast," Darryn said.

Kirk raised a brow. "It's not your turn to cook."

"I think it'd be a good idea."

"Okay." Kirk stood and offered her a hand up. "But you might as well face this head-on, Darryn. Three weeks is a long time to keep your head in the sand."

"I don't know what you're talking about," she said, ignoring his hand.

He stood in front of her as she rose, blocking her movement. "You damn well know what I'm talking about."

She felt the heat from his body. She wanted very much to disavow what he was saying, but with him so close, she was afraid her voice would quake. She forced her gaze to move up his chest, over his wide soft mouth, to his eyes.

"I don't know." Her voice came out breathy.

Kirk gave her a slow smile, his eyes warmed with understanding...or suggestion. "That's a big tent you're using for just one person, Darryn. Kind of a waste of space, don't you think?"

All the warmth left Darryn in a rush. She was struggling with emotions she didn't understand, and Kirk seemed to be experiencing nothing more than physical desire. She felt as if he'd slapped her, then dunked her in a snowdrift.

"No, Kirk," she said with all the hauteur she could muster. "I think it's exactly the right size for me. I have no intention of sharing it with anyone, least of all a rutting grizzly."

That night Darryn regretted her words.

The climbers returned to camp early, long before they were expected. Darryn wasn't surprised. Through the binoculars she'd used to help her sketch them on the climb, she'd seen them start down. From where she sat at the foot of the mountain they had looked near the peak—at least close to where the peak disappeared into the clouds.

The men were cold and tired and disgruntled. Kirk had demanded that they give up an attempt at the summit because the dropping temperature, rising moisture in the air, and mare's tails in the sky warned him of a severe impending storm. Though they could have spent the night uncomfortably but safely on the mountain, he was afraid that the others who'd remained in camp would not notice the storm's forewarnings.

"Worried about the few, *mon vieux*?" Yogurt asked when Kirk explained their early return. "Or do you deprive us of the summit for the one?"

Kirk swore at him. "We wouldn't have summitted in this weather, Yogurt, and you know it!" He strode to the tent to change his clothes.

Yogurt patted Darryn's shoulder. "Do not worry, little one. No one blames you for Kirk's...how you say it?...his immoderate mindfulness of you."

"They must blame me for being here." She gazed forlornly at Kirk's angry gait.

"*Non*, little one." Yogurt shook his head. "We do not. It is a mix-up we have all taken much enjoyment from. Most of these men know Kirk from other years. None of us begrudges him a little...*amour*."

"*Amour*?"

"Ah, *oui*," Yogurt beamed. "Do not pretend to me you do not notice. I am French, remember?"

"Yogurt, that's hard to forget," Darryn said. "But *amour* means love. I don't think that's what Kirk feels at all. Just...lust."

"You Americans are so innocent," Yogurt said, giving her an expression of mock dismay. "Kirk no doubt pretends to himself, and to you also, that he wants nothing more than for you to warm his bed. But I am not fooled, and you should not be either."

He frowned toward Darryn's tent. Because the field where they'd camped was filled with boulders and jutting rocks, they had spread the tents out much farther than usual, seeking soft places in the grass. Yogurt and Darryn stood near his tent, but the one she shared with Kirk was quite a distance away.

"I grant you," Yogurt said, "it may take longer for Kirk to admit it."

"Of course it will," Darryn said, her gaze following his. "Since he doesn't feel it."

"No, little one," Yogurt said. "Because he admitted it once before and it was a grave error. He loved a woman, Bronwyn..." Yogurt's lip curled. "She came on this trip. The endurance trip. She handled it without trouble. Naturally that raised her in Kirk's eyes."

"To a saint, no doubt," Darryn said under her breath.

"Close." Yogurt rubbed the back of his neck. "When Kirk was a boy, his parents, chiefly his mother, took him frequently into the mountains in California where they lived. He loved it. Then his mother died and his father remarried—a very dependent woman, who did not like to leave the comforts of her home. Kirk's father tried to take him camping a few times, but he was not comfortable in the wild and it upset his new wife too much to be left alone. She demanded that her husband choose between her and camping."

"Oh dear," Darryn said. "He lost his mother and in a way his father too."

"Yes," Yogurt agreed. "And access to his favorite place. As soon as he was old enough, he began to hike and camp alone. He met others who shared his love of mountains and learned to climb from one of them. In college, his only sport was climbing. I believe he had a few...romantic liaisons, but he always pulled back as soon as he believed the woman was becoming dependent."

"He sounds almost as obsessive about that as about climbing."

"More so, I would say," Yogurt said. "Then Bronwyn penetrated his defenses. She was an environmental consultant on contract to a Billings firm for six months."

"Where was she from?"

"New York. Kirk's ultimate concept of horror. But he found he could not live without her. And she could not live in a tent. With his forestry degree, he found a job at the Forest Service that would have allowed him still to spend his summers in the mountains and only have to stagnate behind a desk nine months a year."

"That would be an incredible compromise for him," Darryn said. "Did this Bronwyn understand that?"

"Indeed not," Yogurt said. "She laughed at his suggestion that she live in a 'hick town' like Billings. You understand, this came as a terrible shock to Kirk, though I had tried to warn him many times."

"How did you know, Yogurt?"

"I pay attention to women, little one," Yogurt said laughing. "Of course, Bronwyn swore she loved him, but she refused to marry him unless he would move to New York, where she would get him a job with her firm."

"New York?" Darryn's jaw dropped.

"*Oui*, little one. Can you imagine him there?"

"It would be like slow strangulation for him."

Yogurt took her hand and brought it to his lips. "Do you see why I believe you could grow to love him more than Bronwyn ever did? After six months, she did not understand that about Kirk, yet you know it in less than six days.''

"Yogurt, don't say that." Darryn pulled her hand free and covered her eyes. "I can't love him. I just can't. I haven't known him nearly long enough to love him. And he's...well...Yogurt, I don't want to live in a tent either.''

Yogurt put a hand over his heart. "Unfortunate, little one, but at least you don't want to live in New York.''

Darryn's head spun. She didn't know if what she felt for Kirk could be called love. It certainly felt stronger than anything she'd ever felt for a man before. But Kirk wouldn't fit into her world any better than he had into Bronwyn's.

Billings was fourteen million people smaller than New York, but it didn't even vaguely resemble wilderness. It had traffic and concrete and stoplights all over the place. Suburban developments, cliques, and a cocktail party circuit. She couldn't imagine Kirk in any of that. And she couldn't imagine herself giving it up.

"I hope you're wrong, Yogurt," she said on a sigh. "I hope neither one of us feels anything more than lust.''

"Lust is a good way to start," Yogurt assured her.

During dinner, a dreary meal prepared by Kirk, the climbers remained sulky. When the wind picked up with gusty force, Kirk collected all the lanterns and fuel bottles to store outside the tents to keep them from spilling during a storm and urged them all to anchor their tents more securely. He covered the food supplies with waterproof flies and lashed them to the trees with extra rope.

Darryn suggested they build a roaring campfire and ended up listening to another stern lecture on low impact camping from Kirk while the men sneaked away to their tents.

After Kirk had collected his things from her tent, Darryn took off her pile jacket and clothes to get ready for bed. The cold in the tent surprised her, and she pulled the jacket back on over her nightgown before hurriedly sliding into her sleeping bag.

She lay awake, alone, in the dark of the tent, listening to the wind pick up, wondering if anyone else could sleep in such terrifying noise. The tent poles bent nearly to the ground and sprang back as fierce gusts slapped the tent with the roar of thunder. The floor undulated around her, like a rubber raft in a stormy sea. She prayed she had set her tent anchors properly.

When Kirk's predicted storm struck, snow battered the nylon, sounding like nails trying to rip through her shelter. Darryn feared any minute a gash would tear over her head. With their tents pitched so far apart, and no one to share hers, she felt cut off from the rest of the world, isolated from humanity. Scared.

Why, oh why, had she spurned, with such conviction, Kirk's offer to share her tent? Everyone else at least had someone to talk to tonight, someone to assure him that the storm would pass, that their tents would hold up, that the world would still be there in the morning, unchanged by one little bitty mountain storm.

Everyone but Darryn.

No, she realized, Kirk was alone too. And he hadn't this large tent to protect him from the savage elements. He had only a tiny nylon casing, and that was her fault. Darryn couldn't bear it. What if his bivi sac leaked? What if he hadn't taken enough clothes? If they found him blue and lifeless in the morning, how could she live with herself?

Unfastening the screen and storm flap, Darryn poked her head almost outside and called Kirk's name. Once, twice, a third time. The wind grabbed her words and whipped them away. Kirk didn't answer.

Darryn groped in the dark and found her slippers. She tied the hood of her jacket tightly under chin and braved the storm.

Fat wet flakes of snow, falling almost horizontally in the gale, shrouded all the landmarks Darryn sought. Snow buffeted her eyes and she had to squeeze them nearly shut to see at all. She called Kirk's name again, but he didn't answer. Somewhere above the clouds and falling snow, the full moon shed an eerie light. But it didn't help. In the blinding whiteness, Darryn could see none of the tents, nor Kirk's orange bivi sac.

Suddenly she tripped over something big and soft. Well, not exactly soft, but definitely not as hard as a boulder. And definitely louder and more profane than a boulder too.

"Kirk?" Darryn leaned down and felt along his length. "Please come in the tent. I can't sl-sl-sleep," she hadn't noticed her teeth chattering until she tried to talk, "th-th-thinking of you out h-h-here in all this all alone."

"Son of a—"

"Stop swearing at me and come inside."

"I *am* inside, dammit!" With another oath, he unzipped the top of his sac. "I'm warm and dry. At least I was until I opened this zip... God Almighty, woman, don't tell me you're out in this in slippers and that moronic nightgown!"

Incredibly Darryn had no trouble hearing Kirk over the roar of the storm. While she sought an appropriately withering defense of her attire, he began to swear again. This time action accompanied his words.

With a roar of fury, Kirk unzipped his bag all the way and leapt out. Shoving it into Darryn's hands, he suddenly took off running into the blizzard. Darryn held a hand above her eyes and peered into the darkness. With the wind behind her she was barely able to see, and what she saw horrified her.

At a dead run, in his stockinged feet, Kirk chased her tent, which was tumbling away in the wind. She cringed: her anchors hadn't begun to secure the tent in this gale.

While she stood shivering in the wind and snow waiting for Kirk to return with their shelter, hours seemed to pass. But when he hauled it back to her, Darryn took one look at his fearsome scowl and decided he had accomplished the feat in record time. If her toes hadn't felt like lumps of ice by then, she would have climbed into Kirk's bivi sac and avoided him until morning. Perhaps the morning aft—

Kirk snatched his bivi sac from her hands. "Get in the tent, Langtry."

Without argument, Darryn crawled inside. In the dark, she began trying to untangle the mess by feel. Kirk followed her and pulled his sleeping bag from the dripping bivi sac, which he tossed in the corner.

"I guess it's a good thing you put all the fuel bottles—"

"Not a word." Kirk's voice reverberated with fury. "Don't say a word."

She heard him unzipping things, his wet pile suit most likely, and sliding into his bag. His labored breathing rapidly returned to normal, but Darryn felt his anger as a presence in the tent.

"You have thermal underwear in your pack," he said at last. "Find it, get that wet nightgown off your skin, get back in your sleeping bag and go to sleep, goddammit."

"Will you turn your back while I take off my nightie?"

"In the dark?" Kirk roared. "If you aren't out of it in one minute, I'll take the damn thing off you myself. Do you want hypothermia?"

"Honestly, Kirk," Darryn said. "There's no need to shout. I admit I made kind of a mess of the tent, but you—"

"Darryn," he said, his voice silky with warning. "I don't make idle threats. You now have thirty seconds."

Darryn had an uneasy feeling he meant it. She groped around for her pack, which she discovered under her sleeping bag and the clothes she'd taken off earlier. Fortunately the underwear was near the top and easy to find. Slithering into the pants was no trouble. But even in the darkness she hesitated to remove her nightie to don the shirt with Kirk so close.

"Get at it, Brat."

"Are you sure you can't see?"

"Time's up!"

She heard Kirk loom up, saw a large vague shadow as he came toward her. Darryn gritted her teeth. Hurriedly she turned her back, ripped off her nightie and pulled on the dry thermal top. It felt wonderful against her cold skin, and Darryn breathed a sigh of contentment.

Kirk reached her and ran a hand down her back, from the top of the turtleneck, down her spine, over her bottom. "Okay." He moved his hand along her leg until he found her foot and held it a moment. "Now put on socks before your feet freeze, and get the hell back in bed."

Darryn didn't move. Despite her chill, and the wind still howling outside, she'd felt warmth rush through her at Kirk's touch. She felt safe for the first time that night. Humanity had not deserted her after all.

"Kirk..." She couldn't think of anything else to say.

Actually, that wasn't quite true. Darryn knew exactly what she wanted to say: Kirk, please hold me. Put your hands on me again and warm me up. Let me warm you too.

But she couldn't think of anything she *should* say. So she reached into her pack for her socks. They didn't feel nearly as toasty as Kirk's hand, but they would have to do. She groped around for the opening of her sleeping bag and squirmed inside.

Then she lay in the dark in her tent unable to sleep.

The irony made her smile. Darryn *did* feel better than before. After all, she and Kirk were safe from the storm, though as it turned out they'd been just as safe before. But she didn't feel one bit sleepier, and from the sound of Kirk's breathing, she didn't think he'd fallen asleep either. She still had no light. And she still had no one to talk to—she didn't dare talk to Kirk for fear he'd bite her head off.

Though, when she thought about it, he hadn't sounded nearly as angry when he told her to put on socks as he had when he first crawled in from the storm. Certainly he'd had good reason to get so furious—being wakened from a warm sound sleep to chase a tent barefoot across a rocky field in a blizzard. That would enrage a saint. And the way he'd looked tearing after—

Darryn bit down hard on her lip to fight a sudden rush of giggles. It didn't work. Laughter pressed at her chest, making her lungs ache with the effort to suppress it. She rolled over, pushing her face hard into the down bag. Tears of mirth rolled silently down her cheeks.

"Darryn?" Kirk said. "Are you crying?"

Darryn couldn't answer.

"Darryn?" Kirk said again. "What's wrong? I didn't scare you that bad, did I?"

She tried to tell him she wasn't scared, but her voice came out a laughy sob.

Kirk sat up and reached for her. When he touched her back and realized she lay on her stomach, he grabbed her arm and rolled her over toward him.

"C'mon, Princess," he said, stroking her hair. "I didn't mean to—"

Unmuffled by the bag, her laughter erupted.

"I should have known, you Brat!" Kirk said. "What's so damn funny?"

"Y-y-you," she said, pressing her face into his chest to hide her mirth.

"Me?" He laughed too, less heartily than Darryn. "Chasing your tent, I suppose? You know what I ought to do to you, Brat?"

Darryn laughed harder. Rolling onto her back, she quit fighting it.

Suddenly it was easy to fight. Kirk lay on top of her, his face close enough for her to see through her wide staring eyes, even in the indistinct light of the tent. None of his anger remained. He wasn't laughing hard, nor smiling anymore. His gaze roamed over her face as he wiped lighthearted tears off her cheeks with his thumb.

Though Kirk held most of his weight off her with his elbows, Darryn couldn't draw a proper breath. Opening her lips didn't seem to help either.

"You know what I ought to do to you?" Kirk said again, his voice husky and soft.

"Yes, Kirk, I know," Darryn said, her tone pleading. "So do it. Please."

CHAPTER EIGHT

KIRK'S body stiffened in surprise, then relaxed, seeming to melt into hers, despite the layers of down between them. He laughed, softly, warmly. Gentle as the sound was, Darryn felt it rumble in his chest, felt the tickle of his breath across her cheek.

"The customer is always right," Kirk murmured and his lips covered hers.

Darryn couldn't fight him this time, she'd asked for this kiss: begged for it. For days, she realized as the pressure of his lips urged hers to open, she had longed for him to take her in his arms again, to feel the roughness of his whiskered skin across hers.

Tugging her hands free from the sleeping bag, Darryn wrapped them around Kirk's neck and held him to her as his tongue delved inside her mouth, tasting, probing, stroking. Quivers of pleasure whipped through her body with the fierceness of the wind outside.

Yet despite the incredibly sweet sensations Kirk's tongue and lips evoked, Darryn wanted more. A fire grew low in her belly, making her arch toward Kirk, instinctively seeking fulfillment.

The heat inside her rose, till she could not stay still. Moaning with frustration, Darryn raked her hands down Kirk's back, digging her hands deep into the baffels of his sleeping bag.

"Please, Kirk," Darryn begged, her voice a gasping moan. "Please."

Awash in a haze of desire, Darryn didn't think clearly about what she begged for. She only knew that Kirk was the first man who had ever made her want this way, need this way. She longed to throw aside the cloth and down between them, share everything with him, because her heart told her she could never find the satisfaction she craved with another man.

Kirk lifted his head. "Darryn, Darryn," he breathed. "Easy."

He rolled onto his side, pulling her with him. Tucking her head beneath his chin, he gently stroked her short hair. His hand trembled. She barely heard his heaving breath over the pounding of her blood in her ears.

"I don't understand what happens to me with you," he said at last, his voice still hoarse. "I've guided other attractive women, even beautiful ones. I don't usually haul them into a tent and... ravish them."

Her breathing still ragged, Darryn kissed languidly along his throat, not ready to confront this issue. Her laughter had seemed so lighthearted, their kiss so right. Now Kirk sounded deadly serious.

"Ravishment?" she said, sounding as disappointed as she could with her lungs still working overtime. "That was ravishment? Gosh, I always expected more."

He shook her. "Darryn, be serious for God's sake."

"Kirk," she said. "I don't suppose you usually share a tent with these beautiful women you talked about, and they probably don't usually... well, you know, *beg* you to kiss them."

"You'd be surprised," he muttered under his breath. Then he froze. "What do you mean, you always expected more from ravishment?"

Darryn giggled. "What do you think I meant? My father's a doctor, remember. He led me to believe there was a lot more to this ravishment business than just kissing."

"'*Believe*,' Darryn?" Kirk sounded stunned and more gentle than she'd ever heard him. "Don't you *know*?"

Darryn was grateful darkness hid the color she felt pulsing in her cheeks. "No," she said weakly. "I was waiting for... Well, I don't know exactly what I was waiting for." Before tonight she'd have said she was waiting for a man like Daddy. But that would sound absurd now—Kirk wasn't anything like her father, or any other man she'd ever met.

"You must have been waiting for something awful important, Darryn, to have waited so long. What changed your mind?" He took her head between his palms. "Or did I read you wrong? You *did* say 'yes' just now, didn't you? Yes to me? Your first time—here, in this tent, with *me*? A man you've known less than a week?"

"I know a lot about you Kirk."

He kissed her forehead. "Hardly."

"Enough," she said.

"Why, Darryn?" He spoke so quietly now the howling wind outside nearly swallowed his words. "Why me? I'm not your style at all. Is it just the blizzard, making you want to cling to someone? You can't go back, you know. You only get one first time." His fingers gently traced the outlines of her face. "I understand that's pretty important for a woman."

She stroked her fingers through his hair, as if the blond tangles were the most fascinating thing she'd ever encountered. Certainly it was easier to examine every single hair on his head than to answer his questions.

"I know I'll still respect you in the morning."

Kirk snorted. "Fine, make jokes. That's as good an answer as any. Because one thing I've learned about you, Darryn, if you were sure you'd say so."

"But, Kirk..."

He gave her a last soft peck on the lips. "It's a sweet offer, Princess, and I wish I could accept it, but I can't. It's too...happenstance. You don't want your first time this way."

"How do you know?" Darryn asked, hurt and embarrassed by his withdrawal. "I suppose you do this all time?"

Kirk gave a mirthless chuckle. "If I made a practice of deflowering virgins, believe me, I wouldn't be wasting my breath talking now." He released her and rolled over with his back to her. "I'm going to sleep." He squirmed as if trying to get comfortable. "As if I'll sleep a wink after that."

Darryn shuddered at the loss of warmth. She stared into the darkness on his side of the tent, seeing nothing more than a vague lump. She hadn't meant to anger him. But she wasn't ready to put words to the feelings she had for Kirk. Words would commit her in a way that scared her.

Yet she couldn't deny, at least to herself, the presence of those feelings. They had tormented her almost from the day they met. Until now, she hadn't realized she was also torturing Kirk, something she wanted very much not to do.

But, hang it, Kirk was right: look where she was! A tent in the middle of the wilderness. No plumbing, no central heating, no telephone, no lunches with friends, no nice office for her conventional predictable desk job. Worst of all, no respect from her peers at the comfortable life she had made for herself.

Did any of that matter? It sure as heck didn't right now. She'd been surprised from the first how little she missed creature comforts. But it likely would matter to her a darn sight more when she got back to Billings.

Yet at the moment, respect from her friends seemed minuscule compared to the self-respect she'd gained this week. And compared to the respect she saw glowing in Kirk's eyes, it was less than minuscule. It was nothing at all!

Darryn stretched her arm across the small space dividing them and ran a hand down Kirk's back. He didn't move.

"Kirk?"

"Humph."

"When do you climb next?"

"Day after tomorrow, if the weather lets us."

"A big mountain like this one? Or just a face?"

"A pinnacle. Only three pitches."

Darryn opened her lips to speak but couldn't force the words out.

Kirk rolled over. "Why do you ask?"

She opened her mouth again. "I think I'd like to try it."

Kirk grabbed her and pulled her against him, hugging her so hard she could scarcely breathe. For a long time, he didn't say anything, he just held her.

"I won't let you get scared," he promised. "There's an easy pitch around the east side, with a big ledge to rap from. It's exciting. You'll like it. You'll see."

He continued holding her, gently, making no demands. He seemed to understand, they both did, that they needed more answers before they put any more pressure on each other. Slowly Darryn relaxed. Despite the storm still buffeting the tent outside, in the safety of Kirk's arms, she finally slept.

Kirk tightened the harness straps around Darryn's waist. Then he began to tug at the circular straps that went around her thighs. She tried not to react to the intimate feel of his hands on her, but she couldn't help it. Knowing they would soon tie themselves together with a length of rope, that she would put her life in Kirk's strong hands, made Darryn unable to concentrate on a thing he said.

Then he caught her attention. "Have to loosen these straps around your thighs, Darryn."

"What?" she exclaimed.

Kirk looked up from her legs. "Well, it's Yogurt's belt," he explained. "He's strong, but skinny. And your legs... well, women usually..." He swallowed. Then he grinned at her and stroked a finger along her jaw. "You look beautiful in my climbing tights, Princess. I'd say, oh, a million times better than anyone else on this climb. Don't sweat it."

She fought the urge to smile back at him, though she knew he could see it in her eyes. "My toes hurt."

"Good," he said. "That means your shoes fit. Don't want your feet slipping inside them."

"Socks would be nice."

Kirk shook his head as he continued to fiddle with her thigh straps. "Socks would be terrible. You want to feel the rock."

Darryn sighed and looked up at the jutting granite she had agreed to climb. Though even she could see that her pitch was not as steep as the south face, it still struck fear in her. What had possessed her to try this madness?

Then she looked down at the back of Kirk's head again and knew. She had to understand this sport he loved so much. At least she had to understand why he loved it. Because she could no longer deny to herself how much she loved him.

The night they'd shared her tent, she had let the admission fill her heart. She couldn't even say to herself anymore that it would be much easier if Kirk were a cardiologist. Because she knew that Kirk's work meant as much to him, defined him, as much as her father's did him. They couldn't trade places.

Darryn didn't want them to. She wanted Kirk, loved Kirk—desired Kirk so much it shocked her—just the way he was.

She looked up again and felt dizzy.

"Think how proud you'll feel at the top," Kirk said.

"The top?"

He pointed. "That ledge there about a third of the way up."

Darryn swallowed the dryness in her mouth. "How far is it?"

"Only about eighty-five feet. Half a pitch." Kirk looked at her closely. "Second thoughts?"

Darryn started to shake her head no. "Yes, a little," she admitted.

"Natch," he said.

He slid his hand around behind her neck and squeezed tenderly. Kirk had not shared her tent again since the night of the blizzard, but he'd quit trying to hide his feelings for her.

"Do you see how the top rope works?" He turned her head toward the granite tower. "I've already climbed up and fixed a belay anchor up there. The rope will run from my harness, up the pitch through that anchor, down to you. You can't get hurt. Trust me."

"I do trust you."

"Then let's try it." He led her to the base of the rock and tied the rope to their harnesses. "Remember everything I showed you?"

She gave him a weak grin. "I doubt it. Maybe half. Probably less—just, keep my weight over my feet."

"That'll do." He tightened the rope between them, then pointed down at the rock. "That hold there will support your foot. You watched me climb this pitch. Just repeat my moves."

"Oh, right," Darryn said. "As if I remember."

She put her left foot on a small lump on the face. When Kirk had climbed, he'd made it look as if the rock had a million bumps and ledges for feet and hands. Now it appeared as smooth as her polished aluminum coffee table.

"Remember to shout," Kirk remonstrated.

Darryn felt silly but she did as he said. "Climbing."

"Climb on."

Digging her fingernails into tiny cracks and holding onto mere bulges in the granite, Darryn pressed down hard on her foot and began to climb. The moves felt unnatural—she had to turn her feet at tortured angles on tiny insecure edges or stuff them painfully into cracks. Her hands gripped and slipped and abraded, until they felt like sandpaper.

She never felt safe.

When she began, Darryn had wished the men would all go back to their tents and let her embarrass herself in solitude. But as she progressed, she was glad of their support. They shouted encouragement and advice and pointed out holds.

Oh how she wanted to rest. Her hands and feet merely hurt, but her arms and especially her legs burned from the constant exertion it took to hold onto the rock. She longed to lie down and not put weight on any limb.

Darryn tried to take another step and her leg shook up and down uncontrollably. Fearing the leg would not support her, she froze.

"Sewing machine leg," shouted Kirk. "Try to rest."

"Rest?" she shouted back. "Do you see a bed up here?"

"Curse more, little one," Yogurt called. "It helps."

"Cheat, Darryn," Kirk said. "You've earned it."

"Cheat?"

"Hang dog," he said. "Rest in the harness."

"You mean let go?" Darryn cried. "On purpose? I can't."

"Just put your weight on the harness."

"No!"

Darryn gripped her holds harder, pulling herself against the face. Her weight shifted forward, off her legs, and her feet slipped out from under her.

"Aaah," she shrieked. Her stomach lurched as she fell.

In a split second, the harness caught her, pulling her into a sitting position. Darryn clung to the rope and let herself bump lightly against the rock.

"You're supposed to say, 'falling,' Princess."

"Shut up, Kirk," Darryn said. "Dammit."

"That is better, little one. Not forceful enough yet, but better."

After a few minutes rest, Darryn continued climbing. She felt more confidence in the harness, but the sensation of falling terrified her as much if she'd hit the ground. She didn't want to fall again, or even hang dog. Every muscle she owned tensed for each move as she strained to stay on the rock.

At last, amid shouts of congratulation and clapping, she pulled herself onto the ledge and flopped facedown. She never wanted to move again. The thought of getting back to solid ground filled her with too much dread to consider at the moment. She put her head on her hands, resting, trying to blank her mind.

"Darryn?" Kirk's voice floated up to her. "Are you okay, Princess? You did a great job."

Crawling to the edge, Darryn peered over. She had no idea how high she'd climbed. "Oohh!" she whimpered and jerked back hard against the rock.

Crushing herself against the wall as hard as she could, Darryn began to tremble. The panic she'd held at bay for most of the climb took over. She froze to the rock.

The murmur of worried male voices below her seemed to come from another world, one she would never rejoin.

"Darryn?"

"What?"

"You have to get down now."

"No."

"No?" For once, Kirk sounded at a loss. "Darryn, all you have to do is get over the edge. You won't even have to rap. I'll lower you down if you want."

"No."

"You must go up, Kirk," Yogurt said. "Give me the belay."

The next fifteen minutes passed more slowly than any in Darryn's life. When Kirk's beautiful head finally appeared over the edge, she almost burst into tears.

Crawling toward her, he pulled her into his arms and held her. "You climbed like a master," he said. "What happened?"

Darryn shuddered against Kirk's chest, her terror ebbing hardly at all. "I looked down."

"But you did so well."

"Kirk, please," Darryn gripped his shirt. "Just get me off of here. I can't talk about it now."

"You have to look down some more, Princess. It's the only way."

"Can't I go blindfolded?"

"Like an execution?" He laughed. "It won't be that bad, really. C'mon."

He urged her toward the edge. "Now look," he said, "and keep looking until the panic passes. Get off on what you accomplished, how high you climbed."

"I wish I'd quit at three feet."

"C'mon, I'm with you and Yogurt's belaying you."

With an effort of will, Darryn forced herself to look over. Fighting her initial desire to leap back, she made herself stay and look down until some small measure of calm entered her. Finally she nodded at Kirk.

With his help, she turned around and lowered herself over the edge. Despite her natural tendency to keep clinging to the rock, he got her to stand straight out from the wall.

"Hang onto the rope if you want," he said. "Now just start walking backwards. Yogurt's got you."

Kirk rappelled beside her as she walked, talking to her all the way. When at last Darryn put her feet on solid ground, the thrill she should have felt was buried in a wave of sorrow. The men around her cheered and clapped her on the back. Their excitement for her should have been contagious. She felt none of it.

For she knew with piercing clarity that she would never like this sport. She understood, if only dimly, what Kirk loved. The excitement, the challenge, pitting himself and his puny skills against a vast mountain, just him and nature alone together. The chance, the very real chance, that he might not make it made the victory when he did all the sweeter.

But Darryn had felt only fear and relief when she was done. No satisfaction whatsoever. During the climb, her growing certainty that she would never share this sport with Kirk had intensified her fear. Now it made her want to cry. For she knew that climbing was much more to

Kirk than a weekend hobby. It was a huge part of his life: a part she could never share.

Struggling out of her harness, Darryn cast Kirk an anguished glance and ran for her tent.

Darryn stood in the high mountain meadow watching the Storm Expeditions van appear over the horizon, astounded at how different she felt from the day she had watched it disappear three weeks ago. She was stronger and more self-confident; she had gained the admiration of these men. She had learned a great deal about herself and what she wanted from life.

But she was no happier. For she knew she couldn't have it.

For the last two weeks of the trip, Kirk had behaved toward Darryn exactly as he had toward the men. He'd never denigrated her backpacking skills, had appreciated her cooking, had thanked her for carrying every ounce of weight she took off his shoulders.

But he'd never once taken her in his arms. For that matter, except for their one brief uncomfortable conversation after the climb, he'd assiduously avoided being alone with her at all. That talk had consisted of Kirk assuring Darryn she'd like climbing sooner or later if she went on trying it, and Darryn assuring Kirk she never would.

Finally he must have believed her, for he smiled with so much sadness in his eyes Darryn wanted to cry. "Well, it doesn't really matter," he said. "It's not like... breathing or anything. You can live without doing it."

"But can you?" Darryn stretched a hand toward him.

"No." Kirk squeezed her hand then walked away.

Now Darryn was leaving the most beautiful place she'd ever known, a place where she'd felt more alive than she'd thought it was possible to feel. Worst, she was leaving a man she loved with all her heart, a man like no other, who had spent the last two weeks treating her like another man. She had some intense memories and a fierce desire to see him again in Billings.

A hand touched the back of her neck. Darryn knew without looking it wasn't Kirk's.

"Little one," Yogurt said. "Tell him how you feel."

"He doesn't care, Yogurt."

"Americans," Yogurt muttered disgustedly. "This next trip is our last of the summer. We will have a break then before our fall and winter trips. We will be home much more now and in the winter. You can see Kirk frequently."

"Your winter trips aren't so long?"

"No. A few days. Usually just one climb, or perhaps a weekend of ice climbing."

"Climbers," Darryn said. "Of course."

"Only climbers are dedicated enough to want to try the Beartooths in the winter."

Darryn sighed. "I suppose. Kirk said it was the most beautiful time in the wilderness."

"That it is, little one. But also the most dangerous. I doubt very much Kirk would allow you to come, if that is what you ask."

"No," Darryn said. "I couldn't come on another trip, Yogurt. It's too hard to... fail him."

"Fail him?" Yogurt said. "Because you do not like the climbing? So what? You love him, do you not?"

Darryn's throat closed with an ache of tears. She nodded.

"Then tell him." Yogurt looked as sad as Darryn felt. "Little one, I gave up love for the mountains. I do not wish that pain on any friend of mine. At least give him a chance."

Darryn watched as Kirk went from camper to camper, saying goodbye, urging each of them to return next year. Alex, he also urged to come back in February for a winter attempt at Granite Peak. At last he approached Darryn where she stood away from the group, hoping for a bit of privacy for their goodbye.

Kirk took her hand. "Bye, Princess," he said. "You really are, you know. You lost 'brat' status a long time ago."

"Thanks, Kirk." Darryn swallowed. "Aren't you going to tell me I should come back next year too?"

Kirk shook his head. "I couldn't take it. Kind of like hiking with boots too small." His gray eyes met hers, glistening with sadness. "It just hurts all the time, makes me want the trip to end. I've never felt that way in the wilderness before."

"Kirk, I..." Darryn gulped the words. Yogurt was wrong. She couldn't tell Kirk she loved him, not after what he'd just said. "I want to see you in Billings. In real life."

"See?" Kirk's goodbye grip ended and he dropped her hand. "You think your city is real life." He nodded at the Beartooths. "That's my real life, Princess. We just don't mesh."

"You're wrong," she insisted. "At least give us a chance. I want to see you again."

The van pulled up beside them and a couple climbed out followed by a teenaged girl and boy. The girl, a cute brunette with long permed hair, gobs of makeup, and skintight jeans, ran over to Kirk.

He gave a perfunctory wave. "Hi, Tiffany."

"Oh, Kirk, hi!" Tiffany gushed. She grabbed his hand in both of hers. "I thought about this trip with you all year." She let her lips part and slowly ran her tongue around them. "I missed you. Did you miss me?"

"You didn't miss me, Tiff," Kirk said, gently extracting his hand. "You missed the wilderness. It's an affliction you city people get."

"Oh you're so right," she sighed. "It's just awful in Vegas. I can hardly bear it there, all that neon and glitter. I just *live* for all this nature."

Darryn turned aside to hide a smile. It was clear which part of nature Tiffany lived for. But Darryn's smile faded quickly, for she too wished to live for the very same man.

She stared at the Beartooths, realizing she never wanted to go another year without at least one backpacking trip. But if she never got to see the wilderness for the rest of her life, she would survive. If she never got to see Kirk again, never had a chance to love him, she didn't believe her life would be worth living.

"Kirk," Darryn said. "I really need to—"

"Bob, Mary," Kirk said, greeting Tiffany's parents as they approached. He shot Darryn a glance. "I need to get all this stuff unloaded now, Darryn, so you guys can get back to town right away. Roger has to catch a plane tonight."

Darryn wanted to grab Kirk's hand as Tiffany had done and haul him away for a moment of privacy. But before she could even think about doing so, Tiffany wrapped Kirk's forearm in her determined two-handed grip.

"Oh, Kirk, *I'll* help you unload." She gazed at him adoringly through half-closed lids. "You know how strong I am."

Her father patted her on the shoulder. "She's worked out all year, Kirk, to get ready for this trip."

"No kidding?" Kirk sounded surprised but admiring. "Good for you, Tiff. Okay, help me unload."

Darryn's chest ached as she watched the two of them walk to the back of the van. Kirk was treating Tiffany just as he'd treated her the last two weeks: with nothing more than the polite behavior of a paid guide.

Gathering her things, Darryn walked to the van, stopping only to say goodbye to Yogurt. "Wrong again, Yogurt," she said, fighting tears.

"If you love him, little one, you must fight," Yogurt told her. "But you must accept his life. He will not change." He grabbed her pack and swung it into the van for her. "Bronwyn tried to change him. It hurt him deeply. If you wish to change him, please forget him." He offered her a hand up. "But I hope you will not."

As the van pulled away, Darryn stared out the back window. Tiffany had her hands on Kirk again, this time gripping both his biceps and looking deeply into his eyes, while he adjusted the chest straps on her pack. Darryn wanted to stop the van and insist on accompanying Kirk on this trip, or at least give Tiffany the spanking of her life.

Instead she sat silently, watching the man she loved prepare to take a younger, prettier, adoring woman into the mountains with him, while she rode back to civilization. Alone.

CHAPTER NINE

DARRYN glared at her desk calendar, trying to make the dates go backward. It didn't work. October 14th stared back at her, mocking her.

Kirk had been home for two weeks, the longest two weeks of Darryn's life. He hadn't called her once. Obviously he had no intention of doing so.

Of course, she hadn't called him either, though she had dialed his number repeatedly, wanting just to hear his voice. But when she thought about what he might say—some abrupt explanation of why they couldn't possibly see each other—she hung up.

For the thousandth time, she remembered Yogurt's advice. If you love him, fight for him. If? Darryn certainly had no doubts about *her* feelings. It was Kirk's that were still a mystery to her. Clearly Kirk wished to keep it that way, for himself as well as Darryn.

Why would he want to learn that he loved another woman who could never fit into his life? Which was exactly what Darryn did want to find out—how, loving him the way she did, she could make their lives fit together.

But she couldn't find the answer alone. How did one go about "fighting" for a man who obviously meant to do everything in his power to avoid all contact with her? Certainly not by sitting around, longing to see him and doing nothing about it.

A week ago, Darryn had finished the project for her father's cardiology practice that he'd hired her firm to do. She'd redone the information packets he gave to patients about their heart conditions and the procedures they needed, complete with her drawings of course.

Convincing him that he needed it had not been the easy sale she expected. She'd had to get one of his partners to use her drawings when he explained angioplasty to a patient before Daddy saw the light. Ultimately his practice had paid her firm a nice fat fee, the first she'd brought in entirely on her own.

Her boss had been so pleased he'd urged her to try more free-lancing. But the drawings she'd worked on this past week didn't seem as likely to produce any fee at all, much less a fat one.

Darryn spread them out on her desk. Nine of Kirk climbing, three of them close enough to recognize him, the others taking in the mountains he attempted. One or two of each of the men, and one of each campsite.

Her favorites were seven quick sketches, cartoons really, of how not to go hiking with Storm Expeditions: hikers with maladjusted, misfitting or overloaded packs, blazing campfires leaving scars on the earth, a camper in rollers and face creams dropping tissues behind her, and the one she drew from painful memory: blistered feet. That one portrayed a young woman being ferried out of the wilderness on a litter carried like a sedan chair.

Darryn had enjoyed doing the drawings. The work had helped her think about something besides her silent telephone. Unfortunately it had also kept her mind focused on her trip with Kirk and thus increased the empty ache in her chest.

But she knew how much Kirk cared about low impact camping and believed his message got lost in the long dull lectures he gave the first day. No one paid much attention till he got to the parts about hypothermia and high altitude sickness, the things that could kill them. Her drawings could help Kirk convey something he believed in strongly.

If he ever saw them. And he wouldn't unless he saw her. On a purely business basis, it would be folly to send the drawings through the mail. Only a personal visit could ever persuade a reluctant client to change a negative response to a "yes". A shadow of a smile flickered on Darryn's lips as she thought about the kind of response she really wished to evoke from Kirk.

Firming her resolve, Darryn gathered together all her drawings and put them in a portfolio labelled "Storm Expeditions", just as though Kirk were a paying client. Closing the solid brass fasteners on her Coach briefcase, a graduation present from her mother, made Darryn think about the many contrasts since she'd last seen Kirk.

A briefcase instead of a backpack. Her pink raw silk suit, with the oversize jacket and shoulder pads, instead of hiking shorts and T-shirt. Stockings and low-heeled pumps instead of boots and neoprene socks and Band-Aids galore on her feet. Makeup and air-styled hair softened with conditioner and held in place by gel, instead of . . . the real her? Or was this the real her? Could this her truly mesh with Kirk?

She parked her car at the address of Kirk's office, surprised to discover that he shared office space with the travel agent who booked his trips when he was incommunicado in the wilderness. Clutching her briefcase handle till her knuckles turned white, Darryn pushed open the door and walked over the threshold.

Kirk and a plump gray haired woman stood with their backs to her, talking to Yogurt who faced them . . . and her. She stood hesitantly just inside the door till Yogurt noticed her.

"Ah, Darryn," Yogurt said, a broad smile splitting his face. "Please, come in, come in. You have met Maizie, of course?"

"Actually no." Darryn walked toward them. "We just spoke on the phone."

Maizie turned. "Darryn Langtry?" she said, extending her hand. "I'm delighted to meet you. Yogurt told me how much you enlivened Kirk's trip."

"Enlivened doesn't exactly describe it," Darryn said.

Maizie's grip was firm and friendly, and Darryn returned her smile comfortably, still uneasy about meeting

Kirk's eyes. But she could feel him beside her, not smiling, his gaze on her.

When she heard his voice, she knew without looking he had flicked up his infuriating brow. "Oh, 'enlivened' describes part of it, Princess," he said. "But some other words might give a truer picture."

His sardonic tone slipped during this speech. Darryn looked at him and saw surprise then resignation in his eyes as he raked his gaze up and down her body.

She wished she'd worn something a little less outre to the office today, maybe a simple shirtwaist. Kirk had made only one change in his apparel for the city. He wore running shoes instead of hiking boots, with his jeans and long-sleeved T-shirt.

Though Maizie also wore a business suit, Kirk's scrutiny made Darryn feel overdressed and out of place. Perhaps just in the wrong place. He certainly hadn't said anything to make her feel welcome.

"I have something to show you, Kirk," Darryn said. She licked her lips. "Something we should talk over."

"You have come at a perfect time, little one," Yogurt said. "I was just taking Maizie to lunch. You and Kirk will have the office to yourselves."

"Oh, of course," Maizie said, reaching under her desk to grab her purse. "Kirk, will you watch my phone?"

Kirk frowned at Yogurt. "You two are as transparent as—"

"*Vraiment*," Yogurt interrupted. "We would not deny it."

Before Yogurt hurried Maizie out of the office, she grabbed Darryn's wrist and gave it a friendly squeeze. The door shut behind them with a click.

Kirk continued to regard her unsmilingly. Darryn wanted to grab the hem of her short skirt and tug it down. Or kick off her shoes and sit cross-legged on the floor. Anything to make him stop looking at her as if she had arrived from another planet.

"Well, Princess?" he said at last.

Darryn resisted the urge to say something personal and friendly. Kirk obviously did not wish to invite anything intimate. "I have a business proposition for you."

He nodded. "Okay, let's go in my office."

He strode across the room to a door with "Storm Expeditions" painted on it in small gold letters. Holding it open, he gestured her inside.

Darryn took one step into the office and halted, stunned. The organization skills Kirk used in the mountains must desert him at the edge of the wilderness. There wasn't a bare space anywhere. The room contained two desks, a small conference table, an old couch, two armchairs and a low coffee table. Every surface was covered with books, papers, camping and climbing equipment. Pieces of climbing equipment also hung from the far wall, built of brick.

Kirk put his hand on the small of her back and pressed gently, urging her inside. The touch inflamed Darryn. She didn't want to move, wanted to go on standing there, making him push her harder, until he too reacted to the contact. He must have realized it, for he dropped his hand as if it burned him.

"Kirk." Darryn spun around.

He stood right behind her, she nearly banged into him. He didn't back up and warmth radiated from his body. She could see his pectorals heaving beneath the light blue cotton. Pain shone clearly from his expressive gray eyes, replacing the surprise and mockery he'd let her see earlier.

"Oh, Kirk." She leaned closer, eliminating the remains of the tiny space between them. "I didn't come to hurt you."

"What the hell *did* you come for?" he asked, his voice harsh.

"I..." Darryn closed her eyes. *Fight for him.* "This, Kirk."

She dropped her briefcase with a thud and slid both hands behind his neck. Holding him to her, she stroked her cheek over his softer but still not quite clean shaven jaw, then did the same with her lips, nuzzling and nipping from his throat, over his whiskery chin, to his mouth.

"Ah damnit," Kirk groaned.

Bringing his arms around her waist, he hauled her hard against his chest and crushed her mouth with his. Giving her no instant to adjust, he forced her lips to part and thrust his tongue inside. He kissed her till she had no breath, till her legs wobbled and her hands shook as she moved them to his shoulders, clutching him for support.

His hands on her had far more strength. One remained around her waist like an iron band, keeping her where he wanted her. And where she wanted to be. The other pushed aside the lapels of her jacket, sliding inside to her breast. Cupping it in his palm, he teased her nipple with his thumb, till it hardened achingly, straining against the lace of her bra and the silk of her blouse, wanting more of Kirk's touch. As he forced his knee between hers, Darryn's short straight skirt wrinkled up her thighs, exposing most of her legs.

Kirk lifted his head a bare fraction of an inch. "This, Princess?" he said against her lips, his voice shaking. "Don't tell me you came for *this*."

She heard in his voice, even over his hoarse panting, that he was trying to intimidate her. But he couldn't. Not here, in his arms, where she felt so right. He could scare her on a mountain, but not anywhere he could hold her.

"Yes," she breathed. Her lids fluttered open. "Yes, this is exactly—"

Kirk's already hard grip tightened ferociously, cutting off her words. He swore viciously and let her go, striding away from her to his desk.

Darryn stumbled and grabbed the back of a chair for support. She tugged her skirt down, shifting her hips back and forth to get the hem back in place.

"Darryn!" Kirk snapped. "Can't you compose yourself without all that wiggling?"

Darryn looked up to find him staring at her from across the room. He stood as far away from her as he could get, his fists clenching as he determinedly folded his arms across his chest.

When he spoke again, his voice no longer shook but he couldn't keep the strain out of it. "If that's your business proposition, I'm not buying. You'd better go."

Hiding her hurt, Darryn carefully picked up the pile of books from the chair next to her and put them on the floor. Sliding onto the seat with all the grace she could muster, she sat a moment catching her breath.

"I really do have business to discuss with you, Kirk," she said when she had control of her voice. "I didn't realize how much help you needed until I saw this place."

Kirk looked calmer too but still angry. "It won't work, Darryn."

"You haven't even seen it yet, Kirk. How do you know it won't work?"

"You and me," he said. "It won't work. Look at you." He waved a hand in her direction. "Look at the way you're dressed."

Darryn ran her hands down her lapels. "You don't like this suit?" She met his gaze. "Or don't you like what you think it stands for? It's still the same me inside it, Kirk. This suit just says something about where I work—just like your clothes." She stood and took a step toward him. "It's only a trapping."

Kirk backed up and bumped into the wall. "If you come close enough for me to touch again, Princess, I won't stop with a kiss."

A quiver of desire flashed through Darryn as hot as if he'd touched her. "Promise?"

"Don't joke," Kirk growled, slamming a fist on an uncovered corner of his desk. "Because we still won't make it together. If you want your first time on the floor of an office with a man who won't ever see you again, just keep coming. Believe me, I'll be glad to oblige. Beats lunch any day."

"You're only talking coarse to try to scare me off, Kirk," Darryn said. "It's selfish. And it won't work." But she stopped moving toward him.

"What about what you just did to me?" Kirk asked. "That wasn't selfish?"

Darryn straightened the jacket of her suit. "Well, a little maybe." At a growling noise from Kirk, she held a palm toward him. "Okay, a lot. I'm sorry." A grin tugged at her lips. "Kind of."

She picked up her briefcase and returned to the chair she'd cleared of debris. "Please look at these drawings I brought you." Kirk didn't move. "I promise to keep my hands to myself."

Finally Kirk smiled. A real smile, the kind that transformed his face, softening the satanic look and crinkling up the lines around his eyes. "It sounds like we've had some kind of role reversal here."

"I noticed," Darryn said dryly. "Most men don't protect their virtue with such ferocity."

Kirk crossed the office and pulled up the other chair. Tossing aside a pack and several water bottles in his way, he sat down facing her, so close his knees touched her briefcase. He took it off her lap and placed it on the table behind him. Then he reached and took her hand in both of his.

"I don't want to protect my virtue, Darryn," he said, rubbing her palm with his thumb. "I can't think of anything I'd rather do than make love to you, here—anywhere." He looked up from their clasped hands. "What I don't want is a quick affair that ends with both of us getting hurt. Badly. And that's what would happen."

"You won't even find out."

"I already know."

"You don't." She met his gaze determinedly, her lips trembling. "I'm not Bronwyn. I don't want to live in New York."

Something fierce flashed in Kirk's eyes. "Yogurt has a big mouth." His thumb continued its tantalizing movements. "Where do you want to live, Princess? In a tent?"

"In the summer, yes, if that's where you're living." She wanted to take her hand away to grab his shoulders and shake him silly. But she had agreed not to touch him, and she couldn't bear to end this contact.

"How about kids?" he said. "Do you want kids?"

"Of course I want babies, someday," Darryn said. "Don't you? Babies can go camping, kids love it. You're evading the real issue, Kirk. You don't live in a tent all year. You're just using that to hide behind."

His hand stilled on hers. "Yeah? What's the real issue?"

"You're scared to find out what we really feel for each other. You don't want to find out if it could work." She did pull her hand away to gesture angrily, perhaps fearfully. "You're afraid to commit yourself."

"Damn right," Kirk said. "I've tried it now and then and it's always a mistake. For all their talk of liberation, women don't want a partner, they want a guardian. A daddy." He shook his head. "I can't handle that role."

"You don't know I'm like that."

"The hell I don't," Kirk exclaimed. "You're the classic case. Besides, I'd never fit into your life-style. You think a tent is romantic now. But when it's your only home all summer, you'll change your mind. Then you'd try to change mine."

"You are the most self-righteous, stubborn..." Darryn sputtered to a stop because she didn't want to call Kirk what she was thinking at the moment.

Since she'd walked through the door, her emotions had jerked her from nervousness to shyness to ecstasy to heartache, now to near panic. It seemed idiotic to her not to at least give their relationship a chance. After all, look how close they'd grown under adverse circumstances. Surely if they gave it free reign, their love could grow into something beyond exceptional. At least Darryn knew *hers* would. Kirk hadn't actually admitted he loved her—yet.

"Kirk, I have to go to a dinner party tonight at my parents' house." Darryn considered telling him it was to welcome Peter Thretherwell back to Billings but decided against it. "Will you go with me?"

"You must be joking."

"Not a bit." She turned up her palms. "If you really believe you'd be so out of place in my world, come prove it to me. If it's less gruesome than you expect, maybe it will prove something to you. Either way, it's only one night, a few hours. What can it hurt?"

Kirk's expression filled with sadness. He stroked his callused finger down her cheek. "You don't think it would hurt me to watch what I see in your eyes now turn to indifference? Or worse, embarrassment?"

"You could never embarrass me, Kirk. And if you feel that way about what you see in my eyes, then why have you been hiding the last two weeks, pretending I didn't exist?"

"I'm a realist, Darryn, not a masochist."

Darryn grimaced. "I wouldn't hurt you, Kirk."

"You can't help it."

Darryn regarded him for a long moment. "What if you're wrong? Think what you might be giving up."

At last Kirk's lips slanted into a grin. "I never realized that first day what a stubborn female you are."

"I would never have finished the trip otherwise."

"Probably not." Kirk dragged a hand through his hair. "Okay, I'll go with you to Daddy's party. But promise me this, Princess. When you see that we don't fit, give it up. Please? I can't take much more of this."

"Great," Darryn exclaimed. "It'll be fun. You'll see."

Kirk rolled his eyes. "That's what I said to you before you climbed the wall, remember?"

"This will be much easier than that," Darryn said briskly.

"Dreamer," Kirk muttered under his breath.

Darryn leaned over and picked up her briefcase. "Now will you look at my drawings?"

Forty minutes later, when Yogurt and Maizie returned, Kirk had quit admiring her drawings long enough to agree to look at a whole presentation from her.

"You know, Kirk," Darryn said as she packed up her things and got ready to leave. "If you improve your marketing you'll be able to double your prices for your trips."

Kirk's expression hardened.

Even Yogurt looked dismayed, holding a hand over his eyes and shaking his head. "Exactly Bronwyn's words," he muttered.

Grabbing her arm, Kirk pulled her back inside his office out of earshot of Yogurt and Maizie. "Princess, no matter how much I increase my prices, I still won't make as much as a cardiologist. Even if I did, I wouldn't build a half million dollar house up below the Rims."

"You don't have to, Kirk." Darryn couldn't help the smile that spread over her face as she realized Kirk must have been thinking of her more than he let on, or he wouldn't have bothered to look up her father's address. "I just want you to have a little more disposable income." She patted his cheek. "You remember—so you can date someone back here in civilization?"

Laughing, she planted a quick chaste peck on his lips. "Oh, by the way," she said as lightly as she could manage. "One other thing: the party's formal." With that, Darryn spun around and rushed out of Kirk's office before he could change his mind about anything: the party or her presentation.

CHAPTER TEN

THAT night, Darryn dressed five times for her mother's party. For years, she had understood that Daddy's domain did not extend beyond the hospital. At home, Georgia Langtry set the standards of dress and behavior.

But tonight, though Darryn knew exactly what she should wear to please her mother, she doubted very much that sort of outfit would please her date. It upset her to think this already tense night, when she would introduce the man she loved to the father she adored, might start with negative feelings about her clothes.

But to Georgia, formal meant formal, and Darryn couldn't arrive at her mother's in a denim pantsuit. After discarding several outfits, she donned a simple but elegant midnight blue gown that draped in clingy folds from a lapis and pearl clasp on one shoulder. Her only jewelry was matching lapis earrings. Whatever Kirk thought, at least Daddy would say something nice about her dress, he always did.

The doorbell rang just as Darryn was dabbing on perfume. Thank heavens she didn't still have long hair to blow dry and curl.

When she opened the door, flutters of want tightened her stomach and her heart beat rapidly in her throat. Her mouth agape, Darryn stared at the most impossibly handsome man she had ever seen.

Kirk stepped through the doorway into the light of her foyer. His hair, neatly trimmed, glistened golden and the strong look of his smoothly shaven jaw drew her fingers like iron filings to a magnet.

"Kirk?" she finally managed, stroking a palm over his silky smooth cheek. "You..." Her hand moved to his shoulder and down his chest, feeling another kind of silk beneath her fingers. "Where did you get this tuxedo?"

The suit, a classic black with a maroon cummerbund, fit Kirk perfectly, tapering from his broad shoulders to his slim hips as if it had been tailor made for him alone. The studs down the front of the ivory boiled shirt gleamed the way only real gold could.

Kirk took her hand from his lapel, turned it up and kissed the palm. "I bought it for my sister's wedding—she insisted." He shrugged. "I wore it a few times in New York several years ago. Just often enough to convince myself that one tux would last me the rest of my life." He met her gaze, his gray eyes intensely serious. "I don't plan to have much use for it."

The strong feel of Kirk's hand still holding hers seemed to pull Darryn toward him. Or was she drawn to him in a new way because of his stunning appearance in dinner clothes? She hated the thought but she couldn't help it, she wanted to put her hands all over him, rub her face against his smooth shaven one, run her fingers through his freshly cut hair.

She forced her attention back to the moment. "If you need one so seldom, why didn't you just rent one for the wedding?"

Kirk gave a snort. "My family doesn't rent tuxedos. I wouldn't do that to my sister, knowing she cares about such things." He released Darryn's hand to take her face between his palms. "The same reason I wore it tonight, Darryn. I don't want to embarrass you either." His thumb dragged across her lips. "I'm not brave enough to watch you withdraw from me out of shame."

Her tongue came out and followed the path his thumb had taken. "Never."

He continued as if she hadn't spoken. "But understand, Princess, this isn't me." Kirk gestured at his tux. "I can cover my outside in silk monkey suits, but inside I haven't changed. This kind of scene is not for me, and it never will be. I know, I've tried it."

Darryn let his words sink in and realized Kirk was talking about a great deal more than clothes. "Tried it when?" she asked. "What...what family won't let you rent a tux?"

Turning aside, Kirk picked up the wrap Darryn had tossed on the hall chair earlier and held it for her. "Ever hear of Blakely Kirkwood Industries?" he said from behind her.

"Of course," Darryn said. "So has everyone else in the country."

"Probably the world by now," Kirk said, opening the door for her. "They get more international every year."

As he pulled the door shut behind them, he took her elbow to lead her to his pickup parked in the street. After the miles they'd hiked together, having him guide her down a smooth concrete walk seemed silly. But Darryn liked the feel of his hand on her arm, the knowledge that she could trip in these unsupportive strappy little heels and he would prevent her from falling.

But the sensation heightened her awareness of Kirk's point: she wasn't helpless, look at what she'd accomplished in the Beartooths. Her *clothes* made her helpless. Her outfit was no more her than Kirk's tuxedo was him.

He opened the door of his pickup and helped her inside. "My full name," he told her before shutting the door on her startled stare, "is Blakely Kirkwood Storm, IV."

She tried to regain her composure as he walked around the truck to the driver's side. "Kirk, I don't understand. Do you hate your family?"

"Not a bit," he said, leaning one arm along the back of the seat. "I just hate what they do. For over a hundred years, they've made more money than anyone needs from...raping land. They destroyed who knows how many millions of acres of old growth forest in this country, now they're cheerfully destroying rain forest around the world." His fingers clenched into a white-knuckled fist. "They'll build condos in the wilderness, office buildings where forest used to grow, malls anywhere, but no schools: not enough profit in schools." His jaw clenched too tight for speech.

Darryn reached to cover his fist and he jerked it away. She slid across the seat and put both hands on his jaw. "Kirk, please. Don't turn away from me."

His chest expanded with a long breath that he expelled slowly, letting his shoulders slump as tension flowed out of them. "I don't want to turn away from anyone," he said. "Just from the fruits of something I passionately oppose."

He took her wrists and pulled her hands down from his chin, holding them tightly against the seat. "Every three months, I get a huge check from the Family Trust. I don't own the Trust, I can't give it away, I can't turn off the checks. So I sign them over to organizations like the Access Fund, the Sierra Club or the Nature Conservancy. I want to give a little back—do what I can to preserve what's left of the wilderness my family wants to destroy."

"Not destroy, Kirk," Darryn said. "That's not their goal. They just want to carry on the business they've—"

"The effect's the same." He waved a hand around the cab of his truck. "Look at this," he said. "This truck will take us anywhere we want to go. Is this enough transportation for you?"

Darryn winced under the scrutiny of his gaze. "I'd rather have a car," she admitted.

"Figures," Kirk said. "So would my stepmother. She has a Lamborghini, which my father doesn't like. He has a Ferrari. But they can't take long trips in each other's sports cars, so they have a Mercedes to travel together. And, of course, certain social events require a chauffeur, so they also have a stretch limo. Does that sound sane to you?"

"Uh, it does seem a little excessive."

"Understand, Darryn. I will *never* live that way."

"I understand, Kirk. Of course, I do."

"I doubt it." He shook his head resignedly, but his tone lightened. "Else you wouldn't have drooled all over me when I showed up in a tux."

"Drooled all over you?" Darryn exclaimed. "You conceited ape, I wasn't drooling." She crossed her fingers at the lie. "I was just...surprised."

"I bet you were." Kirk twisted the ignition. "Buckle up, Princess. Even if it does wrinkle that...hot dress."

Darryn stabbed the shoulder harness into the latch. "See, you big phony," she muttered. "You like *my* outfit too."

"Damn right," he said, pulling away from the curb. "I'd like to stop right here and rip it off you." He ran a tantalizing hand down her bare arm. "What little of you it covers."

Darryn tried to respond, but the warmth of his touch brought only a small whimpering sound from her lips.

"But you don't look one bit more gorgeous tonight than you did sitting in my tent wearing that asinine nightgown. That's the way I'll remember you, Princess."

Kirk's words hit Darryn like a punch, they sounded so much like a farewell. Hot tears threatened to spill from her eyes and cover her face with runny eyeliner. With her throat so tight, she couldn't manage to get out the words to tell Kirk about Peter Tretherwell. She had decided this afternoon that she simply had to warn him that Peter would be at the party and why. But she had to get hold of her emotions first.

Haltingly, she gave Kirk directions to her father's house below the Rims. The Rimrocks, Billing's most dramatic landmark, were sandstone cliffs to the north and east of the city, jutting four hundred feet above the valley floor. Just below their crest, Evan and Georgia Langtry's house perched on rock and pylons with an unrivaled view of the city and mountains in the distance. The sand colored dwelling, designed by Georgia, had only two small windows visible from the street. The inside walls of the L-shaped house were almost entirely glass, seeming to bring the magnificent view indoors.

Until her senior year in high school, Darryn had loved her home in Billings's high rent district. That spring, at a kegger on the Rims, two inebriated classmates had fallen off the cliffs to their deaths. Since then, though Darryn did not voice her opinion to her mother, she believed that houses like theirs were an affront to nature. People should build on solid ground.

Kirk parked his pickup in the driveway. "Ah a fortress," he said, shutting off the ignition. "A little smaller than my parents', but the same basic idea. No doubt I can leave the key in the truck because knights in chain mail will shoot intruders from the battlements, right?"

"Funny," Darryn said defensively. "My mother doesn't like to live where other people can see in her windows. She says it's too confining."

"I can relate to that," Kirk said. "But locking yourself in a house with no windows seems pretty confining too. Maybe I should take your mother on one of my trips, show her what unconfining really means."

"She'd probably love it," Darryn said. "But she'll never find that out. She couldn't leave her committees long enough."

Kirk reached for his door handle then hesitated. "You seem kinda tense. Having second thoughts?" He took her hand on the seat and gave it a squeeze. "I'll dress up for you, Princess, but I won't lie about who I am. If you've changed your mind about wanting me at the party, I'll understand."

Darryn stared at this man she loved, awed again by how beautiful he looked tonight. If she never saw him in a tuxedo again, would she care?

"I want you to go with me," she said vehemently. "So much that if you won't, I won't go either. And you'll only have to go through this again next time I talk you into it. And you know I will."

For the first time that night, Kirk's smile looked genuine. "When I first saw you, I knew you were trouble. I just never guessed how much."

Darryn returned his grin and knew the time had arrived. "I'm just nervous because... Well, I should have told you sooner."

Kirk's brow rose so high it disappeared under his hair. "Yes?"

"This party is for... the new doctor. I'm supposed to, um, make him welcome."

Kirk's lips thinned into a hard line. "This the guy who got you to take my camping trip?"

"Mmm hmm." Darryn studied her hands in her lap.

"You wanted to get us together so you could compare us, maybe?"

"No, no, Kirk," Darryn hastened to assure him. "I wanted you to meet my parents. I just thought you should know that they, um, think I'm... interested in... well, *why* they think I'm interested in Peter."

With a sigh of determination, Darryn told Kirk all about the picnic for Peter Tretherwell last month—the champagne, her fascination with Peter, her promise. Kirk sat silently, looking grim.

"But it's you I want with me tonight, Kirk," she finished lamely.

"Why?" He sounded angry. "To bail you out of another mess you've gotten yourself into?"

"No. I learned some things on your trip—about me and my life. I want everyone to understand that. You and my family."

Kirk looked at her hard for what seemed like hours. "Okay, Princess," he said at last. "I'll stay, if only to prove to you once and for all that this will never work. If you'd really changed, you could tell your family without hiding behind me." He raised one broad shoulder in a shrug. "But what the hell—why waste the tux?"

Darryn realized she'd been holding her breath. "Thanks, Kirk."

Georgia had unlocked the front door, so Darryn entered without using her key. As she hung her coat in the hall closet, the door opened again, and Jordan and his very pregnant wife, Nancy, joined them in the foyer. Darryn felt an overwhelming rush of relief at the sight of her brother, an ally, who already knew and liked Kirk.

"Kirk!" Jordan said, pumping his hand up and down. "Great to see you. Did you bring him, Dar? Wonderful." He winked at Nancy. "Mom'll be thrilled."

"Jordan!" Darryn hissed. "Don't tease, please. Not tonight. It means too much to me."

Jordan grew suddenly serious as he introduced Kirk to his wife. "Means too much?" he asked. "You sound like you're bringing Mr. Right home to meet Daddy."

Darryn took a step closer to Kirk and glared at her brother.

Kirk rolled his eyes. "Your dear sister has the laughable idea that after one evening back in the exalted presence of society, I'll see the error of my ways and decide I can't wait to rejoin it."

"Kirk, that's not even close to true and you know it," Darryn said. "I think you'll see that our life-styles aren't so darned far apart."

"Is she serious?" Jordan asked Kirk.

"You could have warned me about her," Kirk replied. "Stubborn streak a mile wide and a bona fide gift for ignoring reality."

"I distinctly remember telling you," Jordan said, "that whatever she sets her mind on, she invariably gets."

The spark of humor dulled from Kirk's eyes. "I don't see how she can do that this time. Surely you agree with me."

"*I* don't, Kirk," Nancy put in. "Not at all." She took her husband's hand. "I doubt Jordan does either if he'll give it some thought."

"I don't?" Jordan's voice came out a croak.

"No, indeed." Nancy gave him one of those wifely smiles that said she knew him better than he knew himself. "Not if you consider all you've told me about Kirk and even half of what you've told me about your mother and Evan."

Jordan pushed his tortoiseshell glasses up on his nose. He looked back and forth from Kirk to Darryn, a smile slowly growing across his face. "You're right, sweet." He threw back his head and laughed. "That sure can't happen here."

"Okay, Jordan," Kirk said. "What's so damn funny?"

"It's no big secret," he said. "When I first met Evan, I was six years old. He was my hero. All he cared about was saving lives. He's still a great doctor, but now..." Jordan gestured at the opulent hallway where they stood "...he cares more about appearances, too. Living with Mom has changed him."

"I don't believe that," Darryn said angrily.

"Of course you don't, Dar. You've always been blind where your Daddy's concerned."

"I am *not*!" she insisted. "Besides what does that have to do with Kirk?"

Kirk put a calming hand on Darryn's shoulder. "I think they're suggesting that you'd have less luck than your mother if you tried to change me."

"Bingo," Jordan said. "Princess Brat, you have finally set your heart on something that may give you just what you need."

"And what's that, you traitorous sibling?"

"A comeuppance." Jordan took his wife's hand and led her down the hallway.

Darryn watched them go before speaking. She covered Kirk's hand on her shoulder. "I don't want to change you."

"Don't you? Better be sure, Darryn." He slid his hand free from hers and waved at the hall. "This doesn't bear any resemblance to a tent."

"This is my mother's house, Kirk," Darryn said, her voice full of calm assurance. "Not mine."

Taking Kirk's hand, she led him toward the party. Despite her deep sense of conviction, Darryn felt pulled in a dozen directions as she entered the living room of her childhood, her hand still in Kirk's, and saw her mother. Georgia stood near the archway to the dining room, chatting with three men, one of whom was Peter Tretherwell.

"Good evening, Mom."

Georgia turned. Her eyes widened to perfect O's as she slowly took in the sight of Darryn with a date not of Georgia's choosing. Finally her gaze came to rest on their clasped hands and stayed there as she crossed the room.

Kirk's fingers wiggled as if trying to get free from Darryn. But she continued to grip his hand, defiantly ignoring her mother's blatant disapproval.

"Darryn, darling," Georgia said. "How delightful you decided to bring a date. Do introduce us."

Darryn did, while casting a look of appeal at Jordan, who took the hint and joined them.

"Kirk, of course," Georgia said. "The mountain man. I would never have recognized you from Jordan's description. He speaks very highly of you. I'm just surprised to meet you outside the wilderness."

Darryn blushed, furious at her mother's condescension. "Oh you'll be surprised, Mom," she said. "He can eat with a fork if you give him a hunting knife on the side and even knows how to use indoor plumbing."

The frown flashed on and off Georgia's lovely face so fast only Darryn caught it. "Don't be coarse, darling."

Kirk took less trouble to hide his irritation. "Yes, *darling*," he whispered under his breath. "I'm your date, not your weapon."

Georgia patted Kirk's arm. "I was just wondering about seating arrangements, now that we'll be nineteen for dinner." Darryn's nostrils flared. Extended, her mother's table easily seated twenty-four. "Of course we have plenty of room, Kirk, I just get all mixed up about uneven numbers."

"Darryn has the same trouble," Kirk said, a sardonic curl to his lips. "One date, two—she can't quite keep track."

Georgia chuckled prettily.

Darryn wanted to slap them both. "I'm sure you'll manage, Mom. Just be sure you put me next to Kirk."

"Don't make things *too* confusing, Darryn." Georgia's smile didn't waver but Darryn recognized the underlying sharpness in her voice. She wondered if Kirk did. "I have you next to Peter. He's the guest of honor."

Darryn met her mother's steely blue-eyed stare unflinchingly. "Another night perhaps."

Georgia recognized when the bounds of politeness were about to be violated. "Of course, dear, that would be lovely. Don't worry about your father being disappointed." With a small nod at Jordan and Kirk, she left them.

Kirk grabbed Darryn's bare arm and tugged her around to face him. "Lighten up, Princess. I thought you two might come to blows any second."

"It did look fierce, Dar," Jordan said. "But it sure as hell made my point about appearances."

"I never said appearances meant nothing to Mom," Darryn said. "That's why I insisted—I want her to understand how much I've changed." She narrowed her eyes at the archway where Georgia had disappeared. "I wonder how she'd feel if I told her Kirk and I shared the same tent in—"

"Don't even think it," Kirk growled, "unless you want to walk home. There's no reason to intentionally hurt your mother's feelings."

"Dar," Jordan said. "You should have rebelled in high school like all the other kids. Don't try to make up for it all in one night."

Somewhat subdued, Darryn led Kirk toward the group of doctors surrounding her father, who stood somewhat apart talking shop. When Darryn introduced Kirk, none of them, least of all Evan, showed the slightest surprise at his occupation. Her father changed the subject to the last wilderness bill introduced in Congress.

Kirk sidestepped a political debate and soon had the group laughing over stories of Darryn ending up on the wrong camping trip. When the others drifted away, Evan tried again to draw Kirk out.

As the conversation turned serious, someone touched Darryn in the small of the back and she spun around to find Peter Tretherwell, tall, handsome, expensively dressed as always. Biting back a demand that he not touch her without her consent, she forced a smile. His provocative dark eyes smiled back at her.

"Hi, gorgeous," Peter said, putting a possessive hand on her head. "What happened to your long blond locks? Did you and Davey Crockett there chop each other's hair in the wilderness? Jordan tells me he's never seen his hair so short."

Darryn shook off his hand. "Hi, Peter," she said. "I got a haircut to make the camping trip easier."

"Ah yes," Peter said. "Our camping trip. I was afraid you'd forgotten your promise, when I've thought of nothing else for seven weeks."

"Noting else?" Darryn asked dryly. "What about your med boards?"

"A mere distraction from the thought of you and me alone in a tent."

Darryn laughed in spite of herself. "What nonsense, Peter. I grew up with a doctor, remember? No woman could possibly compete with boards."

"No woman but you and the thought of sharing a tent—"

"We won't share a tent, Peter," Darryn interrupted. "We'll just take a day hike."

"I've already gone out on a limb with your father," Peter said, "demanding four days off my first week. He agreed only because you were going with me. Didn't want to disappoint his daughter." He leaned closer, speaking in more intimate tones. "You *did* promise. And Evan assures me, you'll be the perfect guide."

Darryn lifted a glass of champagne from the tray of a passing caterer. More likely, Daddy didn't want her to disappoint Peter. Evan had reminded her again just yesterday how important it was to make Peter feel at home in Billings so he'd stay with the practice. Wasn't that really why she'd come to this party? To please Daddy by welcoming Peter?

"Well, you'll have to bring your own tent. Mine is a one man tent and—"

"Exactly what I had in mind, gorgeous. You and one man in your tent." He gave her a friendly leer, wiggling his eyebrows wildly.

Darryn laughed again, though less heartily. Peter's flirting was heavy handed enough to seem harmless. Still she felt uncomfortable encouraging him. Obviously she must have done so the night of the picnic, though she couldn't remember clearly because of all the champagne she'd drunk. But no matter what she'd said then, she certainly didn't want to lead him on further tonight.

She looked at the glass in her hand now, surprised to see it already half empty. Well, it *was* making her more relaxed.

"I'm serious, Peter," she said, no longer sounding quite so stiff. "Two tents."

"Whatever you say, gorgeous," Peter agreed, running his soft palm down her forearm. "You're the leader."

Darryn removed her arm from his touch. Had he truly been this forward at the picnic? Unfortunately she believed he had, and she had enjoyed it. Even a man like Peter, a man so used to getting his own way, wouldn't act *this* familiar if she hadn't let him think she invited it.

"Something wrong, Princess?" Kirk asked coming up behind her.

"Not a thing, Davey," Peter said.

Darryn introduced the men and tried to move off with Kirk before the two of them engaged in conversation. Peter stopped them.

"Your princess here was just telling me what I'd need to bring on our camping trip next week."

"Was she really?" Kirk raised both his brows at Darryn. "You plan to go camping alone with him *this* time of year?"

Darryn opened her mouth, then shut it again. She couldn't explain in front of Peter that she was going only to please her father. "Kirk, I..."

"The chance of a killer storm this late is too high," Kirk said firmly. "Even without one, it could be dangerously cold. You don't have the experience for winter camping."

Nervously, Darryn lifted her champagne glass to her lips. Kirk caught her wrist. With deft movements, he took the glass from her fingers and deposited it on a table.

"That stuff gets you in trouble, remember?"

"Kirk," Darryn whispered heatedly. "Don't tell me what to drink, for heaven's sake. Can't you drop this? I'll explain later."

Kirk smiled at Peter. "Ask her again next spring. In the Beartooths, that'll be late June at the earliest."

Peter gave Kirk a mock salute. "Thanks for the advice, Davey. But I think Ms. Langtry is old enough to make her own decisions."

Darryn suddenly felt like a piece of raw meat, caught between two circling vultures. She didn't expect more from Peter, but Kirk's behavior shocked her. Could he really be jealous? Or was he just being bossy out of habit? She wanted to say something caustic to him, but she wouldn't dream of doing so in front of Peter.

Besides they were *both* acting disgustingly infantile, so she settled for telling them both what she thought. She was glad Kirk had kept her from drinking more and spoiling the biting clarity of her voice.

"When the two of you get home to your kennels tonight, I hope you both understand why your beds are cold and lonely." She took a step back. "And likely to remain that way."

Georgia slipped an arm around Darryn's waist. "Dinner is served, darling. You're on Kirk's right, just as you asked. Peter's on your other side."

Darryn leaned back against the plaid seat covers in Kirk's truck, relieved to have escaped from the party before midnight. Dinner had been awful, with Peter vying for her attention by constantly baiting Kirk. Peter's mannerly killer instincts led him unnerringly to the subjects Kirk cared most about: the wilderness, rain forests, the environment.

Kirk's deep ingrained tact avoided an argument of ballistic proportions. But his reserve had given Peter free reign to mock concerns Kirk held dear. Darryn had done all she could to stop Peter's alcohol-laced gibes, without much success. Mostly she had longed for this moment, when she could again be alone with Kirk.

"What an ordeal," she sighed.

"You said it." Kirk started the truck. "I hope I proved my point."

"By behaving like a gentleman?"

"Me, a gentleman? Hardly. Your doctor friend acted like a gentleman, keeping the conversation light and amusing. Taking things as seriously as I do is considered quite barbaric."

"Kirk, if you'd responded to his nastiness, my mother's dinner would have been a disaster."

"Exactly. That's why us barbarians avoid those situations." He backed out the driveway and headed toward her condo up Alkali Creek. "Though in terms of bar-

barism, your father takes the prize, throwing you to the wolf that way.''

''He's not—''

''What would you call it? Expecting you to take that lecher camping in unstable conditions. It's insane.''

''Peter's harmless, Kirk. He's just... Well, he's brilliant, he went to Harvard, he's a doctor: he's probably used to women falling at his feet. But he's far too civilized to do me any harm.''

''Civilized?'' Kirk scoffed. ''That animal?''

The motion of the truck, her release of tension from getting away from Peter, was making Darryn sleepy—too sleepy to argue. More, the contentment she felt being alone with Kirk filled her with joy. Never in her life had she ever felt so comfortable with anyone.

Yogurt was right, this sort of felicity was worth battling for, but not with sharp words and fists. Darryn would fight a softer way, but with the tenacity of a heat-seeking missile.

''I love it that you're so jealous, Kirk.''

''I am *not* jealous,'' Kirk insisted. ''I have no claim on you.''

''You do, you know. I love you. That gives you some say in who I—''

''You do not!'' Kirk pounded his fist on the steering wheel. ''That's a completely irresponsible remark. You've only really known me three weeks. And your parents despise my chosen profession.''

''They'll come around after we're married and have a dozen children.''

''Darryn, we are *not* getting married. It wouldn't work.'' He turned up her street. ''You handled the camping trip well, but that doesn't mean you're really ready to turn your back on your world.'' He shot her a rueful glance. ''The only time you've relaxed with me is when we're alone.''

''Not true, Kirk. Tonight was a bit awkward, but it was Peter who made me uneasy, not you.''

"Hah!" Kirk said. "All we'd have is a great time in the sack."

"Mmm," Darryn murmured, "I'm glad you noticed." She put her hand on his thigh. "We also have intellectual and emotional communion, Kirk."

Kirk snorted. "Did you get into the champagne again when I wasn't looking?"

"We do," she persisted. "We can talk about anything, we agree about the wilderness. Heaven knows, we like kissing each other. You desperately need my organization skills in your business. I'll do your marketing and you'll make twice the money and be glad to have me." She smiled dreamily. "It sounds idyllic."

"Must have been *stronger* than champagne," Kirk muttered, but he didn't push her hand off his leg.

He parked in front of her building and turned on the seat to face her, one arm resting on top of the wheel. "If we had what you say—if you feel what you claim— you wouldn't even consider going camping with that gorilla."

Darryn slid closer to Kirk along the bench seat. "I told you at the party but you wouldn't listen. I'm only going because Daddy asked me to. He wouldn't do that if anything bad could happen to me."

"How the hell does he know?" Kirk demanded. "Even if this alleged human acts like a perfect gentleman, which we both know is unlikely, the weather could kill you. You're going into the Beartooths!"

Darryn snuggled up next to Kirk, hoping to end this argument with a kiss. Kirk took her shoulders and put her away from him.

"If you go, take a guide who knows enough about winter camping to keep you alive."

Darryn shivered as he held her away from his warmth. "Oh that would go over big," she said. "Whose tent would you share—mine or Peter's?"

A muscle twitched in Kirk's cheek. "Take Yogurt then."

"Yogurt!" Darryn giggled explosively. "Oh heavens no. Kirk, you know how I feel about my father. He's given me everything, and he almost never asks anything of me. I'm sure it'll be all right. He loves me."

Kirk's fingers clenched tighter into her shoulders till she wiggled them in pain. With an oath, he opened his door and climbed out, hauling her after him. He did not release her arm but led her at a trot to her door.

Sticking out his hand, he muttered, "Key."

"Don't I get a good night kiss?"

He stood like a stone. Darryn's cheeks burned at his refusal. At last she dug in her bag for her key. Kirk took it from her, unlocked her door and pushed her inside.

"Goodbye, Daddy's darling," he said sarcastically. "I bet *your* bed is cold and lonely too, and Daddy sure as hell isn't going to warm it for you." Grabbing her wrist, he turned her hand palm up and slapped the key in it. "If I were your Daddy, I'd warm something else."

The door slammed behind his back.

CHAPTER ELEVEN

DARRYN put out the flame beneath the feather-light stove she'd borrowed from Yogurt, wishing again she'd had the sense to borrow Yogurt in the flesh. What on earth had ever made her doubt Kirk?

Though no snow threatened from the black star washed sky, the temperature had dropped to well below freezing. Darryn longed for the comfort of her thick down sleeping bag a few feet away. But she was afraid to enter her tent for fear Peter would follow.

Unfortunately Kirk had been right about Peter too. All day, he'd behaved like a gentleman, as charming and witty as ever, till Darryn felt foolish for ever letting Kirk convince her she had anything to worry about. Then during dinner, Peter's words became slurred and he seemed to grow eight hands, each of which he wanted to put somewhere on Darryn.

She'd shrugged him off, laughed him off, shouted him off, slapped him off. She'd said no a hundred different ways. Nothing had deterred Peter for more than a minute or two. He stopped his advances only to take more pulls at whatever he had in his water bottle.

He moved toward her now in the dark of the moonless night. "C'mon, gorgeous," he said, clutching at her heavily. "It's freezing. Let's do this inside the tent."

He hauled her close enough for Darryn to smell liquor on his breath. She wondered how much he'd brought with him and when he'd started drinking it.

"We're not going to do anything in the same tent, Peter." Darryn fought to keep her teeth from chattering. "You get in your own and leave me alone."

"You think I hiked all this way up here to sleep alone?" Peter crowed. "Forget that, babe." He pulled

her toward him, pressing his wet lips over her face.
"Mmm, tastes good."

She struggled, arching her head away from him. "Stop
it!" She tried to twist away as he bit along her throat
but his hand on her jaw held her fiercely. "No, Peter!"
She slapped at him. "Stop!" One hand connected
sharply with his cheek.

Peter swore and jerked his head back. "Okay, babe.
We'll do it that way."

He grabbed her arms, twisting them behind her back
and pressed her to the ground. Her breath whooshed out
of her as he landed on top of her with all his weight.

"Peter, no!" She struggled uselessly. "Your repu-
tation...my father...won't...the practice." She couldn't
draw enough breath to speak clearly.

Peter chuckled with revolting confidence. "You think
they'll care? Those old men need me too damn much,"
he said. "They'd never say anything to hurt their precious
practice."

"I will!"

"The hell you will." His whiskey breath nauseated
her. "Your Daddy won't let you." He laughed his disgusting laugh again. "Now be a good little girl."

He gyrated his pelvis painfully up and down on hers,
while pressing his knee hard between her thighs. His
weight on her chest grew heavier.

Feeling as if she would strangle, she dragged a full
breath into her lungs and let out a piercing scream no
one would hear.

Suddenly she was free. Gasping for breath, she sat up
and peered at a dark swirl from which came the ugly
sounds of fists meeting flesh, Peter grunting and
swearing. Then, miraculously, came the beautiful sound
of answering oaths in Kirk's enraged voice. More
punches landed. Peter's grunts turned to incoherent
groans.

"Kirk, stop!" Darryn cried.

A second later, Kirk scooped her into his arms. A lump she barely saw but assumed was Peter lay on the frozen earth, moaning piteously. Darryn snuggled tighter to Kirk with every noise Peter made. His arms, strong and warm around her, filled her with comfort and the assurance she was safe.

He stood, still holding her, and carried her to her tent. "You'll have to crawl inside, Princess."

She nodded and he put her down. Inside he pulled her back into his arms.

"He didn't hurt you?" Kirk said, half questioning, half reassuring.

She shook her head against his chest. "No. I...I should have listened to you, Kirk."

"None of that," he said, gently massaging the tension from the back of her neck. "Not now."

She couldn't understand why Kirk wasn't angry with her. "But you—"

"Don't worry, Princess." Kirk pressed a finger to her lips. "We have seven miles to hike tomorrow. I have every intention of lecturing you all the way home." His fingertip slid back and forth over her lips. "I might even work up a good mad. But not now."

Darryn relaxed. Now that she knew Kirk hadn't turned into a saint, she realized she vastly preferred his gentle comforting to a lot of "I told you so's", which she would undoubtedly have to listen to tomorrow. Tonight, she would take what he offered, gladly.

She hoped he would not offer more. His arms around her, his breath in her hair, his finger on her lips, all felt wonderful. But she couldn't face anything else tonight. The very thought of Kirk's lips touching her where Peter's whiskey laced saliva had defiled her seemed repellant.

Kirk must have understood for he made no demands. He removed her boots and helped her into her bag. When he had crawled inside his own, he pulled her into the crook of his body and held her tight.

Just as she was falling asleep, Kirk called, "Get into your sleeping bag, Tretherwell, or you'll die of exposure tonight. Not that we'd miss you."

Darryn fell asleep too fast after that to know if Peter complied. She couldn't bring herself to care if he did.

In the morning, cold woke her. The part of her body inside her bag felt warm, but her nose and ears ached. Daylight shone brightly through the tent. The thought of seeing Peter made her ill and she prayed Kirk had already made him leave. Hoping that was why he had let her sleep so late, she crawled outside.

There was no sign of Peter. Kirk sat alone by a fire. Darryn was shocked. He never scarred the earth with a fire.

He must have read her mind. "I thought you'd need the warmth this morning. It's on a fireproof sheet. It won't leave a mark." He offered her his rolled sleeping bag to sit on. "Coffee? Do you want something to eat before we start back?"

In the cold bright morning, a terrifying awareness of what Kirk had rescued her from rushed into Darryn. She began to shake all over.

Kirk uttered an oath she'd never heard him use before as he came to her and wrapped her in his arms. "He can't hurt you, Darryn. He won't come near you again. I promise. If you want, I'll ... I'll kill him."

"Oh that's a nice offer." Darryn giggled. "Is that part of your guide service?"

"Yeah. Just for princesses." He tucked her head into the crook of his neck. "Princesses and brats."

"Oh?" Darryn felt her strength returning as Kirk's teasing calmed her spirits. "And which one do you think I am this morning?"

"This morning you're all princess." His chest expanded against her breasts as he pulled in a long breath. "But you wouldn't be here if you weren't part brat." His tone grew more serious as if his teasing words had hit too close to the truth. When he spoke again, his voice, though still tender, had lost any hint of laughter. "Better eat or you won't make it down the trail."

While Darryn drank a cup of coffee and ate a bowl of Kirk's almost burned oatmeal, he packed her bag and took down the tent. Despite Darryn's protests, he put it into his pack. He wouldn't even let her wash the dishes. He scraped out the bowl and pot and shoved it all into his pack.

When he had the fire thoroughly out, he dumped the wet ashes into a pit he'd dug about a foot deep and covered it with the hunk of sod he'd lifted. Darryn looked around at their camp. Humans had left no signs except the torn grasses and stirred earth where Kirk and Peter had fought.

She shuddered as the memories assailed her again. What would have happened to her if Kirk hadn't come along? Why wasn't he telling her something to that effect now, at the top of his voice?

His silence made her nervous. She didn't look forward to a seven mile tongue lashing, but she would prefer it to this brooding. In the long run, his seething would turn to anger. Rather than wait for his temper to heat to boiling and erupt, she wanted the argument over with now.

"Aren't you going to say, 'I told you so?'"

He shook his head, his eyes dull with sadness. "It wouldn't do any good." His tone was flat. "You can't change."

"Change?"

Kirk didn't answer, he simply held her pack for her to slip into. "You lead," he said. "Set the pace as slow as you want. You've got plenty of daylight."

Except to offer her drink or food, or ask if she needed rest, Kirk didn't say another word to her until they reached the trail head. Though she started the hike at a snail's pace, her awareness of Kirk's increasingly bad mood behind her chivied her into picking up the speed within a mile or so. Soon she hadn't enough breath to speak herself, much less try to get him to talk.

At the trail head, Darryn remembered that she'd come in Peter's car. In the gathering dusk, she spotted Kirk's pickup and leaned against it to catch her breath. "I guess...I need a ride." She kept her gaze on her boots. "Would you mind?"

"Not at all." Kirk could have been speaking to a rock.

He took the key from under the front bumper and unlocked the door on her side, holding it open for her without a word. On the drive to her condo, he answered her desultory questions with polite smiles and few words.

"Kirk," Darryn finally said. "I've changed my mind. I want you to kill Peter."

"What?"

"Not really," she said, as he pulled to a stop in front of her condo. "I just wondered if you were still alive in there." She grabbed his forearm before he could leap out of the truck. "Please talk to me. You weren't angry last night. What happened this morning to make you so mad?"

"I'm not mad, Darryn." She wished he'd call her Princess again. "I just know what you want, and I can't give it to you. It hurts. It hurts a lot, I'll admit. But it shouldn't surprise me. I knew it from the beginning. We don't fit."

"What do you mean, you can't give me what I want? Do you think I'm so materialistic? I don't—"

Kirk was shaking his head. "I wish that was all it was. You want a daddy, someone to bail you out of one disaster after another." He dragged a hand through his hair. "By the time I got a copy of your trip plan yesterday, I had to run all the way up the trail with that damned pack on my back."

Darryn cringed with remorse. "I should have told you where I was going, I know that. But you acted so...negative about it. I just told Yogurt."

"Wrong again, Darryn," Kirk shouted, pounding hard on the steering wheel. "You shouldn't have told me where you were going. You should have listened to me and stayed home!"

Darryn held her hands toward Kirk. "You're right this time. How can I argue with that? I'm sorry you had to run seven miles uphill."

"The hell you are," he growled. "If I'd walked even another couple of yards, I wouldn't have gotten there in time. Do you know what I thought when I heard you scream?" He closed his eyes in a tormented grimace as if he could hear it again and wished he couldn't. "I've faced more life threatening situations than you can imagine, but I have never been as scared as I was running up that trail, listening to you scream."

Darryn reached toward his cheek, wanting to feel his flesh, his stubbly growth of beard, beneath her fingers. Kirk grabbed her fingers in a viselike grip and wouldn't let her touch him.

Darryn's throat ached from the lump of tears that had gathered where her voice box ought to be. "I love you, Kirk," was all she could get out.

"You just love the idea of me. Someone strong like your Daddy, who'll carry your pack, rescue you from disasters, tell you where to hike, with whom. You got too old for your Daddy, now you want me." He shook his head, clenching her hand so tight she thought her fingers would break. "I've seen what a dependent woman does to a man. I won't let it happen to me."

Without another word, he got out of the truck and began to unload her gear. Darryn leapt out and tried to take her pack from him, but he wouldn't let her. Handing him her key, she slumped onto the bumper and quit fighting the tears that rolled down her cheeks.

When Kirk returned, he slammed the back cover of the pickup, shutting out the overhead light and leaving them in near darkness. "Did you want me to carry you inside, too?"

Darryn dashed tears away with her fist. "No, Mr. Storm, I wanted you to carry me over the threshold. But I guess you don't have the strength."

"Don't have the strength?" He sounded incredulous. "Me?"

"Not where it counts, in your heart." She poked his chest with her index finger, once, another time. She wanted to pound on it with both fists. "You are the worst kind of coward. You hide your real fears behind big muscles and adrenaline stimulating sports, so you can tell yourself how macho you are. Then you never have to admit to yourself that you're scared of anything. But you are. You're an emotional coward. And it won't make you a happy old man, Kirk."

Sobs muffled her last words. Her vision blurred as she ran for her door. Inside she kicked aside her camping gear and fell on her couch, planning to cry herself ragged. But she couldn't. Emptiness assaulted her: in her heart *and* in her apartment. It seemed to echo from the walls.

She had never before feared being alone in her own house, but now memories of Peter made her tremble. Kirk's reminder that no one was there to help her only increased her fright. She leapt up and ran to her door to make sure she had locked it. Just as she reached it, a knock pounded on the other side.

Darryn screamed.

"Darryn!" Kirk shouted, rattling the doorknob.

Darryn jerked open the door and fell into his arms. He stroked her back and held her tight.

"I just thought you might want me to check your apartment for you," he said. "I'm sure it's all right. You're really sure too, if you think about it. But I'll check it if you want."

Darryn didn't say anything.

"Do you want me to look?"

She nodded. "I want..."

"You want what?"

Her voice came out small and muted by his fleece jacket where she hid her face. "I want you to stay the night."

Kirk groaned and his arms tightened around her. She felt his instinctive hardening and she snuggled tighter into his embrace.

"I can't, Darryn."

"Please."

His hands began to caress her body, almost as if he had no control over them. They feathered her hair, massaged her bottom, stroked up and down her spine.

"If you're afraid, Darryn, I'll stay on the couch." His hands came to rest at last on her waist. "I can't let passion answer this question for me. It's not a decision to make lightly."

"Don't you want me?" Darryn whispered into his ear. Her lips touched the whorls, and she breathed warmly, feeling shudders overtake Kirk.

"Brat," he said, landing a smack on her bottom that only pressed her closer against him. "You must enjoy seeing me suffer."

He took her head between his palms and kissed her lips, quick and hard. Darryn felt that he meant to pull away but she slipped her hand behind his neck and held him to her as she traced the line of his lips with her tongue. With a moan, Kirk opened his mouth, thrusting his tongue deep inside her.

Darryn clung to him, feeling safe in his powerful arms, even as surges of passion sapped her strength, leaving her muscles and bones so ineffectual they barely kept her standing. The yearnings Kirk roused in her stormed through her body with the stunning power of a high mountain storm.

Though Darryn would have given herself to Kirk in their tent, and even in his office had he asked it, tonight she felt more completely his. In every cell of her body, in the deepest chamber of her heart, in her most female core, she understood that only Kirk would ever know this part of her. For no matter what he believed, the first time Darryn said yes to him, she committed herself to him, and she did so for life. She would become a woman with Kirk or she would not do so with any man.

Kirk moved her toward the couch, lowered her onto it, and laid himself over her. Her head tilted back as he nibbled kisses along her neck to the pulse at the base of her throat. Darryn began to moan, clutching at the back of Kirk's head, tangling her fingers tightly into his hair. Her body arched against him, frantically seeking union.

Gasping with hoarse breaths, Kirk fell to her side. Turning her back to him, he hauled her into the crook of his body and held her immobile while they calmed.

"You don't want it this way," he said at last, his breath still coming hard.

"Oh yes, I do." She struggled to face him but he wouldn't allow it.

"I mean to leave in the morning," he said into her hair. "Do you still want me to make love to you? Think hard before you answer, Darryn. Because I can't resist much more of this."

Darryn crumpled inside. She wished her body would crumple with her emotions. But she was not so lucky. Desire still held her fiercely in its grip, spreading waves of heat and a throbbing ache where she longed to know Kirk. But her heart seemed to sigh, its beating diminish. He was right, she did not want a one-night stand.

"No."

His arm relaxed from around her waist and he struggled to a standing position. Pressing her shoulders down on the couch, he kissed her nose platonically.

"I'll check the apartment. If you still want me to stay, get me a pillow and blanket for the couch."

When Kirk returned, Darryn had straightened to a sitting position. She leaned forward with her hands clasped between her knees.

Kirk came to her. "Did you decide?"

She nodded. "I'll be all right."

He gave her a sad smile. "I thought you would. You know my phone number if you need anything."

She nodded again, unable to speak.

Kirk stood for a moment. "Bye, Princess." He turned to go.

When he opened her door, Darryn felt as if that black square of night outside was swallowing her last chance of happiness. "You wouldn't be so sad, Kirk, if you didn't love me. You wouldn't have chased me up that trail, you wouldn't mind leaving me now. You certainly wouldn't refuse to stay the night with me."

As she spoke, Kirk's shoulders grew rigid and his knuckles turned white on the doorknob. But he didn't turn. "I said it hurts, Princess. It hurts like hell."

He closed the door quietly behind him.

Darryn awoke stiff from sleeping on the couch, where she had cried herself to sleep. Trying not to think about the painful emptiness in her heart, she rose and showered. A glance in the mirror showed her eyes still puffy and red.

She had to tell Daddy about Peter Tretherwell, and she might as well get it over with. Today was Sunday. He wouldn't have surgery scheduled and they could have a long talk.

She didn't feel like putting on makeup. But Daddy wouldn't like to see her with the marks of her crying so obvious. When he heard her story, he would suppose Peter had caused the tears. That might make him angrier at Peter, which Darryn wouldn't mind, but she didn't want Daddy to think she cared enough about Peter Tretherwell to have wasted tears on him. With a sigh of resignation, she donned makeup and a corduroy jumper and turtleneck.

Not surprisingly Evan was making rounds when she phoned him. Since she rarely bothered him at the hospital, he assumed something was wrong, and he offered to meet her right away. Darryn said lunch in his office would be soon enough and she'd bring the sandwiches. When she arrived at the submarine shop nothing looked good. She bought Evan's favorite and a large cappuccino for herself.

Evan opened his clinic door to her knock. Taking Darryn's shoulders, he held her where he could examine her carefully. "You look terrible. What's happened? Is it a man?"

"In a way, Daddy. In a way, it's worse."

He ushered her into his private office and the two of them sat in chairs in front of his desk. Evan ate while Darryn told him of the trip with Peter. Wishing him to understand her terror, she did not skimp on details. Halfway through the story, Evan put down his sandwich and just listened.

"Thank God," he said, when she had finished, "that Kirk came along when he did."

"Thank Kirk," Darryn amended.

"Of course." Evan looked anguished. "It's my fault. This never occurred to me—not from Peter. I should never have urged you to go."

"It's true I went to please you," Darryn said. "But it's not your fault your new partner turned out to be a rapist."

Evan looked startled. "That's a little strong, isn't it, sweetheart?"

"I don't think so." Darryn put her untouched coffee cup on Evan's desk. "If Kirk hadn't arrived when he did, that's exactly what would have happened. And if he hadn't been so strong—"

"Pfaugh." Evan cut her off. "That's hardly true, dear. You know a surgeon would never allow himself to be drawn into a fistfight and get his hands bruised. Peter has surgery scheduled this week. He was defenseless against Kirk."

"Defenseless?" Darryn jumped to her feet and began to pace. "What about me? What about when he was on top of me, trying to force me? Who was defenseless then?"

Evan rose and took Darryn's hands. "Sweetheart, of course you're the one who suffered the most. And I understand completely why Kirk acted as he did. I would have too."

Darryn felt chills down her spine as she stared at her father, hearing the compassion in his voice. She had heard it so often before when he spoke to patients, she had no idea how much he meant it now. A minute ago, he'd expressed compassion for Peter Tretherwell.

"Wouldn't it have bruised your hands, Dad?"

Evan still held her hands gently but a frown creased the smooth skin between his brows. "This is no time for sarcasm."

"What are you going to do about this, Daddy?" she asked coldly. "Call the authorities or just tell Peter to leave the practice?"

Evan's hazel eyes widened in astonishment. "Call the authorities? Darryn, do you have any idea what that would do to this practice?"

Darryn tried to free her hands, but Evan held them tight. "What will it do to your practice to have a rapist for a partner?"

"I don't believe Peter can be called a rapist. He simply had too much to drink and got a little carried away." Evan pulled her toward his couch and forced her onto it. "You've had a terrible experience," he said soothingly, patting her wrist with a gentleness she found appalling. How many times had he used this tone on a terrified patient? "Of course, you're frightened and upset. When you've had a chance to calm down, you'll realize that making this public would only increase the harm that's already been done."

Sagging limply, Darryn quit fighting her father's ministrations. But something inside her died. "You aren't going to do anything."

"There's nothing to be done," Evan said again. "I'm just grateful Kirk happened along when he did."

"Kirk 'happened along', Dad, because he loves me." Darryn let out a long sigh. "But not as much as I love him."

"I'm sorry to hear that," Evan said.

"You're sorry to hear I love him?" Darryn asked.

"No," Evan said, "though I wish you'd chosen someone whose life-style was closer to your own."

"Like Peter Tretherwell, brilliant surgeon and molester?"

Evan winced. "I admit I thought Peter might be a perfect mate for you, before this happened. But that's not what I meant at all."

Darryn traced a welt around the cushion on which she sat. "What did you mean?"

"I hope you're wrong that he doesn't love you as much as you love him." Evan pressed his fingertips to his temples. "Perhaps you've noticed over the years that I did exactly that with your mother. I'm not sure she'd have had me at all, if she hadn't desperately needed support and a father for Jordan. She was in pretty dire circumstances when I proposed."

Darryn's gaze snapped up to her father, catching the look of pain on his face. "Mom loves you."

"She does now," Evan agreed. "More than when we married, certainly. But not the way I love her. The love of Georgia's life was her first husband. When he died, that sort of love perished for her forever." Evan turned up his palms. "I knew that, but I loved her so much I thought it would be enough for both of us. It does things to a man to spend his life trying to please a woman who will never return his feelings. I don't wish that for you."

Darryn swallowed. "Jordan was right. He said Mom changed you." She stood, feeling utterly defeated. At the door to his office, she turned. "If it weren't for Mom, would you call the police? Would you kick Peter out?"

Evan shrugged, sadness darkening his expression. "I can't say, sweetheart. I've considered her wishes first for so long, I don't know anymore what I do for her and what I do for myself. But you must know that sort of public attention would destroy your mother."

Darryn nodded, feeling sorrier now for her father than for herself. Crossing the room, she hugged him. "I love you, Daddy. No matter what." She kissed his cheek. "Did you like Kirk when you met him?"

"Very much." Evan smiled. "In fact... Well, I already had Peter in mind for you, which I see now was a mistake. But I remember thinking how good Kirk had been for you. That perhaps a man like that, a man who would care for you without..." he looked at her, deep affection bringing the shadow of a smile to his lips "...spoiling you rotten, might be just what you need."

"Spoiling me?" Darryn pretended incredulity. "Surely you don't mean to suggest that I've been spoiled by my father?"

Evan laughed. "If the shoe fits..."

Darryn forced a sort of chuckle, though it didn't contain much cheer. "Well, you certainly needn't worry about Kirk spoiling me, rotten or otherwise." Her lower lip began to tremble and she bit it. "Actually you don't have to worry about him at all. He won't have me."

"Young men," Evan said disgustedly, shaking his head in disbelief. "He'll have you, Darryn. He's just fighting the inevitable. But, sweetheart, believe me, you shouldn't have him unless he loves you more than you say. More than life itself." He touched her cheek. "The way I can see you love him. Otherwise, you'll never find the happiness you deserve."

"I'll keep that in mind, Daddy." Darryn turned to go. "But I love him too much to turn him down...if he ever asks. No matter how he feels about me."

"If he doesn't love you that much," Evan said as she opened the door to leave, "he's out of his mind."

In her car, Darryn sat gazing out the windshield at the Rimrocks for a long time. The thought uppermost in her mind was: *Daddy is human*. All her life, she had placed her father on a pedestal, considered him nearly a god. Now he had toppled. Worse, far worse, than the imperfections she saw in him, were the imperfections she saw in his life. It hurt her deeply that the Daddy she loved so much had never found real happiness. She wondered what he'd have done with his life if he hadn't spent so much of his energy trying to please Georgia.

And Georgia! When Darryn fought down the irrational fury she felt at her mother for hurting Daddy so badly, she realized that Georgia deserved more pity than he. She had spent the main part of her life trying to substitute social position and material possessions for love. What a dreadful unhappy choice.

Darryn shuddered, knowing how close she'd come to making the same sort of choice for equally bad reasons. Yet she couldn't help a fresh surge of anger when she realized what her mother's influence over Evan—and Darryn—would result in now.

The knowledge that Peter Tretherwell would suffer not at all for his vile actions, would go on being considered a brilliant young surgeon, respected in the community, sought after by unmarried women, made her ill. More nauseating still was the knowledge that Peter would get away with it merely because adverse publicity would upset her own mother.

When she was ready to scream, Darryn thought of Kirk, of his reaction to her near rape: He wanted to kill her attacker with his bare hands. His strength, his natural reaction unblemished by politics or personal gain, made her love grow inside her till she thought she'd burst with it.

Suddenly, as if a cartoon light bulb had flashed on over her head, Darryn understood what Kirk wanted from her: just what he wanted that first night in her tent, when he had thrown away her makeup and pronounced her natural coloring more beautiful. He wanted her unqualified love, untarnished by social conventions and material yearnings. He needed to believe, to know in his heart, that she loved him just as he was, rough, unshaven—determined to make his own life without his family's wealth.

Oh, Kirk, Darryn thought. *You may look hard to everyone else, but I've seen your soft inside, and you don't fool me*.

She wanted to cry. No wonder he'd gotten so upset every time she mentioned money. He thought she wouldn't want him if he didn't make more money, when all she really wanted was to be able to take the summers off and spend them with him in the wilderness. Would he ever believe her now? Could she convince him their worlds didn't have to fit, because she knew her happiness would come from doing whatever it took to fit into his?

With a new determination to assure him of her love and hopefully at last give up her innocence in the process, Darryn stuck her car into gear and headed for Columbus, the small town about forty miles from Billings where Kirk lived. She had looked up his address as soon as she returned home from the backpacking trip, trying to picture the place where Kirk lived in civilization.

His house, a small cream colored frame dwelling with forest green shutters, looked dark when she arrived. His pickup was not in the driveway, nor...Darryn peered through the garage windows...in the garage. She pounded on his door and received no answer. Noticing the flag up on his mailbox, Darryn flipped it open, praying he'd left her a letter explaining his absence. Instead she found a letter from Kirk to Maizie, addressed to her at home.

Desolated, Darryn drove back to the interstate. At the fast-food restaurant near the entrance ramp, she stopped for coffee. Spotting a pay phone, she responded to impulse and called Maizie at her home.

"I think that letter's just his trip plan," Maizie said after Darryn had explained. "He called me early this morning and said he'd mail it to me. He and Yogurt are attempting a winter climb of Mt. Bern."

"But there's a storm coming," Darryn wailed. "I just heard it on the radio."

"I know," Maizie said. "I heard it too. But Kirk and Yogurt didn't know about it. They left before dawn."

"Dear heaven," Darryn said, her voice trembling. "How long a climb is it? When will they be back?"

"Why don't you come over and I'll show you on a map?" Maizie said. "In fact, why don't you pick up that letter of Kirk's too. It'll probably give more details."

At foolish speeds, Darryn returned to Kirk's mailbox. If that letter contained any information about Kirk's whereabouts that Maizie didn't already have, Darryn wanted it now. A blizzard was coming.

As she headed back toward Maizie's, snow began spitting from the prison gray sky. Wind threw the flakes hard against her windshield. She tried not to think of Kirk and Yogurt outside in this weather, perhaps caught on a sheer rock face helpless to escape the blast of a subzero storm. Swallowing her terror, Darryn kept driving.

CHAPTER TWELVE

WHILE Darryn sipped the hot spiced tea her hostess insisted she needed, Maizie read Kirk's letter.

"He doesn't say much about the climb. Just gives a more detailed description of his route than the one he gave me over the phone." She folded the letter and returned it to its envelope. "Just the usual: the number of the Ranger station, what time to expect them out and what time to panic and call in the cavalry. Things like that."

Darryn put her cup down. "That's all?" she asked forlornly. "Nothing about...me?"

"There's quite a bit about you, in a way. Not that he meant to be so revealing." She patted the envelope. "You can read it yourself. Though you should know...it may hurt to read it. Do you still want to?"

"Yes!"

"I knew you would. But I want you to understand something first." She poured herself a cup of the spicy tea. "I've known him a long time. Since before..." she glanced at Darryn. "You know about Bronwyn?"

Darryn nodded. "Yogurt told me."

"Before Bronwyn, Kirk dated quite a bit, though he was picky. And clingy women scared him off." Maizie blew on her steaming tea. "Since that witch, he hasn't dated at all."

"She really broke his heart."

"I don't think so," Maizie said. "He didn't love her that much, not nearly as much as he thought. But his experience with her convinced him that no woman could be trusted, ever."

"Hasn't anyone tried to change his mind?" Darryn asked, dismayed.

"Of course." Maizie returned her cup to its saucer and leaned back against the plump sofa cushions. "Yogurt and I. But we didn't try very hard until recently because there was no...incentive."

"I'm the incentive?"

Maizie smiled. "You're more than that, as you must know. But you have an uphill battle with Kirk. You...any woman...starts out in his mind with two strikes against her."

"I must have had six."

Maizie nodded. "From what I've heard of your trip, at least the beginning, that may be true." She held out the letter. "I hope you two work it out. Kirk's been absolutely foul to share offices with since he got back this fall."

Darryn grabbed the letter, pulled it out of the envelope, and began reading. She saw at once what Maizie meant when she said the letter wasn't really about her but that Kirk had revealed more than he'd meant to. He'd written Darryn's name dozens of times up and down the margin, then scratched it out.

Fear kept Darryn from doing more than scanning the details of the climb. Her gaze caught only on his explanation of the last pitch before the summit: "We can't stop here, impossible to bivi, no way to down climb. If the weather requires a bivi, we'll have to summit before we can dig in."

Darryn's heart stuttered at the words. "If the storm hits them on this last pitch, they won't be able to get out of the weather."

Maizie nodded. "Not until they reach the top."

"They'll get cold and wet." Darryn's voice rose. "They'll freeze before they can set up their tent."

"It's a risk," Maizie agreed. "But the storm should hit today, and they won't reach that pitch until tomorrow. I doubt they'll even attempt it."

"You're sure?" Darryn couldn't keep the anxiety out of her voice.

"No, not positive. If the snow stops by morning, who knows what they'll do? But they're wise climbers, they won't go on unless the conditions are good."

"Whatever that means."

Darryn read on, squinting to read the last paragraphs which Kirk had also crossed out more than once—but not so thoroughly that she couldn't make out the words.

You can tell, of course, this trip is Yogurt's idea. Last minute and everything. Not my style, but I need to get out of town. You know why. Someday I may find a woman I can call a mate, one who'll stand on her own two feet and tolerate my life-style. But I doubt it. My life-style is too demanding. Besides it hurts too much to look.

Not that I looked for this one. She blindsided me. And I doubt there's another like her in the universe. Which is probably lucky for the universe. But maybe not for me. You can spend the next two days preparing your big lecture, Maizie, but don't give it. I tried this time, I really did. Wore a tux, went home to meet Daddy, all of that. But she never found a place for me in all the other essentials in her life that I could tolerate.

Damn it to hell, Maiz, I didn't expect her to give up silk suits. Just put me at the top of her list.

Kirk's words ran out there. He hadn't signed the letter, just stopped writing. Darryn kept staring at the crossed out words, in too much pain to cry. Tears would do no good. She had to make Kirk believe she understood.

Darryn now saw her camping trip with Peter the way it must have appeared to Kirk. Not only had she put Daddy's wishes above Kirk's, but she'd also let her mother and father convince her that making Peter welcome was more important than following Kirk's sound advice about winter camping. They had spoken of social conventions, he had talked about saving her life.

Worst of all, she had completely ignored Kirk, the man she loved, when he asked her not to go off alone with another man. The memory made Darryn cringe. No wonder Kirk didn't believe she put him at the top of her list.

But she did, she did. Where else would her heart put Kirk but first? She knew that now, understood it in the marrow of her bones. She would make Kirk believe her if it took the rest of her life.

Darryn filled her lungs with a determined breath. Kirk had said she was stubborn—he had only the tiniest inkling of how stubborn she could be. But he was about to find out, now that she truly understood what mattered in her life. She imagined proving it to him could have some very pleasurable moments.

With a lonely howl, wind threw an eddy of snow against the window. Darryn's head snapped up. She forced herself to meet Maizie's uneasy gaze.

"I'm scared for him," Darryn said. "Yogurt too."

"Me too, sweetie." Maizie rose and went to a credenza on the side of the room. "Like something stronger than tea?" She opened a door and pulled out a bottle of brandy.

"No thanks," Darryn said. "I think it would make me sick right now. And I'd probably do something dumb. Kirk thinks it gets me in trouble."

"Does it?"

"Well, only a couple of times," Darryn said. She drank another sip of tea but it had cooled too much to soothe her. "I think I'll go home, Maizie." She folded the letter she had crumpled in her tight grip and returned it to the envelope. "Can I take this?"

"Sure. I'll just write down the numbers." Maizie poured a snifter of brandy and took a big sip. "Just what the doctor ordered."

Picking up a notepad and pencil, Maizie held out her hand for the letter. Darryn still clutched it and somehow could not bear to release it. She opened the letter herself and read the phone numbers and times to Maizie.

"So," Maizie said, her voice a little too bright, "we'll hear from them by three tomorrow."

"We hope," Darryn said. "But he said not to call until six. Why?"

"They're often late. Climbing isn't an exact science. When they register for the climb at the Ranger station, they agree to pay for a helicopter if they're more than two days late. It costs a fortune." Maizie turned up her beautifully manicured hands. "They don't want us, me, to panic too early."

"Their lives are worth a few thousand dollars, for heaven's sake!"

"Of course they are," Maizie said. "But it'll ruin their credibility too. Crying wolf." She tapped the pages. "This is just a backup. They don't expect me ever to have to call anyone. They've done this an awful lot, Darryn, and come out fine every time without *ever* needing help."

Darryn drew a long breath that didn't seem to get to the bottom of her lungs. Something, fear no doubt, was restricting her breathing. "Okay, I won't panic," she lied. "I'll call you tomorrow at three."

Maizie gave her an understanding smile as she walked Darryn to the door. "Sure. And I'll call you if I hear anything. I promise. In fact, I'll make that thick-skulled Kirk call you. How's that?"

"Wonderful, if he will." Darryn stuck her arms into her coat. "I just wish I'd had a chance to talk to him before he left. I wish he knew how I felt."

Maizie patted her hand. "That'll make his homecoming more fun. Don't worry, you'll get a chance to tell him." She gave a suggestive smile, wiggling her carefully drawn eyebrows. "And show him, dahling."

Darryn giggled and hugged Maizie. "Thanks." Stuffing the envelope in her pocket, she left.

* * *

Stopping at Jordan's, Darryn borrowed back country ski gear and listened to a long lecture on its use. Halfway through, when Jordan seemed to be repeating himself, Darryn stifled a yawn, realizing how often her brother had gone on and on like this when he thought her safety was concerned. So had her father.

No wonder Kirk thought she was spoiled. Or had Daddy said that? Maybe all of them had. It wasn't *her* fault they'd all treated her like a piece of delicate porcelain. But she'd never tried very hard to stop them. Until now. Darryn felt as if she was coming out of a cocoon, a loving but very confining cocoon.

"Jordan, I get it," she said. "I can't learn anything else from words. I have to get out on the snow."

"When do you plan to do this, Dar?"

"Not until Kirk shows me how," Darryn said, "unless I have to."

"What do you mean 'have to?'" Nancy asked.

"Well, he and Yogurt are climbing Mt. Bern now, in this storm."

Jordan snorted. "No way. They're retreating as we speak, count on it. Besides, do you think *you're* going to rescue them? Don't even think about heading up that trail alone." He sounded *so* authoritative, almost pompous.

"I don't want to," Darryn said. "But I just want to...cover all contingencies." She reached for the double boots to try them on.

Jordan grabbed her wrist. "I mean it, Dar. Promise me you won't go up there alone."

Nancy shifted her unwieldy body in the armchair as if she couldn't get comfortable. "Jordan's right, Darryn. You don't know what you're doing."

"I won't do anything foolish," Darryn promised. But, she vowed silently, she would let her heart decide what was foolish.

Nancy stood and sat down again. Then she stood once more and began to walk slowly around the living room.

"Is something happening, Nancy?" Darryn asked excitedly.

Nancy rubbed back and forth across her distended middle. "I don't know. I'm not having contractions. I just can't get comfortable."

Darryn rose from her spot on the floor surrounded by ski gear and gently hugged her sister-in-law. "I hope so. I hope it's a beautiful little girl who will try Jordan's patience as much as I've always done."

Jordan laughed. "No one could beat you in that area, Dar." He put an arm around his wife. "Can I do anything?"

"Yeah," Nancy snorted. "Birth this baby for me."

"I won't leave you, sweet." He looked excited but nervous. "I know who did this to you."

Feeling like an intruder, Darryn began scooping up ski gear. "I'll see all *three* of you tomorrow."

Jordan pulled his gaze away from Nancy. "Let us know the minute you hear anything."

Darryn agreed and left with her arms full of equipment she hoped she never had to use.

Darryn clamped the double boots into the back country bindings, just as Jordan had showed her. She wished he was with her now, but Nancy had gone into labor at ten this morning, and Darryn hadn't wanted even to give him a hint of what she had in mind. Her brother would be otherwise occupied for some hours to come.

The Ranger had dismissed her frantic call, since he couldn't schedule a helicopter before daylight and he wouldn't send a search party till he had an idea where to look. The Sheriff hadn't been much more enthusiastic about looking in the dark and cold and snow for a man who taught wilderness survival. But Darryn had finally convinced him that a man like that wouldn't be six or seven hours late unless something was seriously wrong.

"All right, all right," he'd finally muttered. "I'll call the Search and Rescue. It'll take 'em awhile to get everything together."

"I'll probably get there first."

"Don't you start up that trail without us, young lady. We got enough people to look for. Hear?"

"I can't wait anymore, Sheriff." Darryn tried not to sound impudent, just adamant. "I won't go far, not past that fork where the trails divide."

"Young lady," the Sheriff said again, more sternly. "That's seven miles into the forest."

"The storm has stopped and I have warm clothes," Darryn said. "If you see my car at the trail head and I'm not in it, I'll be on the trail."

"Know where you'd be if you was my kid," he muttered. "We'll be right behind you on snow machines."

Hoping "right behind" meant just that, Darryn skied across the snow packed wooden bridge over the frozen creek and started up the trail. Forest Service markers nailed to trees shone clearly in the moonlight. The trail rose gently at first, and she had no trouble manipulating the randonnee bindings. The mohair skins Jordan had glued to the bottom of the skis kept her from sliding backwards as the trail grew steeper.

Less than a mile into the forest, the trail narrowed and tree branches brushed against her, dropping their snow covering silently by her feet. The quiet and beauty of the forest, lit by a full moon, convinced Darryn that Kirk was right: the wilderness was most beautiful in the winter. Though she longed for the snow machines to appear behind her, she understood they would ruin the repose of the forest.

Soon the trail became so steep, Darryn got no glide at all from her skis. With the snow as deep as her thighs in places, she did little more than plant a ski, let it slide backwards till the skin caught, then press up on it. Her breathing grew labored, but she didn't consider stopping.

She longed to pull the ski mask off her face for a full breath of air, but she knew better than to do that either.

Hiking last fall with a full pack on her back had taken less effort than this. She wished she had that pack now, at least a power bar and a bottle of carbohydrate replacement, instead of the water she'd brought with her. She gulped some without slowing down.

The trail markers seemed farther and farther apart. Most likely it was just taking her longer and longer to get from one to the next. She stopped a moment and listened, hoping to hear the Search and Rescue coming up the trail behind her. No sound disturbed the deep quiet of the forest.

"Oh, Kirk, where are you?" Darryn panted plaintively, forcing her burning thigh to lift her ski up the trail one more time.

"Little one?" Yogurt's voice in the dark sounded stunned. "That cannot be you, can it? I hallucinate, yes?"

"Yogurt!" Darryn cried. She tried to rush forward, but the deep snow slowed her. "Where's Kirk?"

Yogurt came toward her, his progress maddeningly slow. "Kirk is here." He gestured over his shoulder at the sled he was towing. "Do not tell me you are alone. You could not be so foolish."

Briefly Darryn wondered how many more men would lecture her today. "The Search and Rescue are coming behind me. Soon, I think. What's wrong with Kirk?"

"He broke his ankle early in the climb."

"Broke his ankle?" Darryn struggled forward again.

"A good thing, for we turned back. When the storm hit, we had already descended and could bivi at once."

Darryn pushed past Yogurt and dropped awkwardly to her knees beside the small plastic sled he towed. Yogurt had strapped Kirk's arms to his chest, but his legs dangled off the back.

"Kirk," she said, pushing the mask off his face. "Kirk, Kirk." Snatching off her own mask, she kissed

his cheek, his lips, feeling his chilled skin. "Yogurt, he's
cold as ice and not responding. I'm sure he's in hypo-
thermic shock. We've got to get him warm."

"You are right, little one." Yogurt dropped his pack
to the ground and began digging inside it for the tent.
"He went into shock earlier, from the broken bone I
believe. That is why I decided to bring him out this
afternoon instead of waiting for morning. But he was
still conscious last time I checked. I do not believe that
was long ago."

Yogurt had the tent up in minutes. With a folding
shovel, he leveled a place in the snow to pitch it. Moving
more quickly than she'd have thought possible in his
snow gear, Yogurt removed the sleeping bag from his
pack and got it laid out inside.

"We must get him inside the bag, strip his clothes off
and our own, and put him between us for warmth."

"We won't all three fit, Yogurt. I'll do it." Under other
circumstances, Darryn would have protested taking off
her clothes in front of Yogurt even in the dark. But she
knew there was no other way to revive Kirk and if they
didn't do it quickly, he could die.

"I'll go first," she said, "so that when we get his
clothes off there'll be something to warm him right
away."

As she undressed inside the bag, Yogurt removed the
outside of Kirk's double boots and got him into the tent
and into the bag beside Darryn. Between them, they
managed to get his clothes off. Darryn was shivering so
hard herself by then, she was afraid she wouldn't have
enough heat to give him. But as she wrapped her arms
around him and pulled his cold body against her own,
she realized Kirk's skin temperature had dropped
dangerously. Frightened, she pulled him closer, touching
him everywhere she could.

Yogurt cocked his head as they heard the welcome
roar of a snow machine coming up the trail. "Stay with
him, little one. I will direct the Search and Rescue."

Darryn managed a terrified smile. "What else would I do, Yogurt, run down the trail naked?"

Yogurt chuckled and left the tent, leaving behind a small flashlight, casting eerie shadows on the nylon walls. In minutes, Darryn heard voices outside and an unpleasant motorlike noise at the entrance to the tent, which began to warm slightly.

"We shall leave this heater for you, little one," Yogurt said, holding open the tent flap a moment, "while we prepare a sled to get Kirk down the trail."

"To get us both down, Yogurt. I won't leave him till he's in the hospital."

"Good," Yogurt said. "I think he needs you."

A minute later, Yogurt returned and covered them with more blankets while the men outside created a big enough sled to carry two of them. Kirk began to shiver violently.

"He is warming," Yogurt declared, feeling Kirk trembling as he patted blankets around them.

The trip down the trail probably took less than an hour, but it seemed to take days. Before she was safely in a warmed four wheel drive with Kirk still beside her, Darryn was nearly frantic.

During the drive, Kirk's lids fluttered and he tried to speak but his voice was slurred and he could barely form words over his viciously chattering teeth.

Darryn kissed his face, his eyes, his lips, again and again. "Don't talk," she murmured. "Just shiver. It's good for you."

"H-h-h-heav-v-ven," she thought Kirk chattered.

"Heaven, you idiot?" she said, pressing her cheek to his icy skin. "You nearly died."

Kirk moved his shaking hands over her chilled undressed body. "He-he-heaven," he said again.

Evan met them at the emergency room. "Just here visiting my granddaughter," he explained in response to Darryn's question. "They told me you two were coming in to Emergency." He turned to a nurse. "Let's get her in a tub of warm water and something hot to drink."

He examined Kirk and tried to get him to respond to questions. "He'll need a warmed IV and heated blanklets before we can treat his ankle."

"Daddy, *I'm* fine," Darryn said. She grabbed his arm and pulled him close to her lips. "I just need my clothes and I have no idea where they ended up."

Her father patted her cheek. "Then you'll have to do what you're told, won't you? You're both spending the night here." He nodded to the nurse. "Get her in a tub."

"Honestly! Daddy, wait," Darryn called as her father turned to leave. "How did Nancy do? What did she have? What did they name it?"

"Nancy did just fine," Evan said. "I hate to tell you what she wanted to name that beautiful little eight pound girl."

"What?"

"'Darryn'. Can you believe it? Fortunately Jordan convinced her that one Darryn was almost more than the family could handle."

Darryn felt tears burning the back of her lids. "How sweet. But I'm glad my niece didn't have to go through life with a man's name. What did they choose? Jordina?"

Evan laughed. "Caitlin."

"Beautiful," Darryn sighed.

"Here's your ride," Evan said as a nurse arrived with blankets, a robe and a wheelchair.

Though still protesting, Darryn allowed herself to be wheeled away.

At last, when Kirk was warm, his foot casted and resting on a pillow, everyone else left room. Darryn pulled her chair as close to his bed as she could get it and leaned her brow against his hand which she had firmly clasped in both of hers.

Except for a few affirmative grunts at his doctor, Kirk had said almost nothing since Darryn entered the room. Now he tugged hard on her hands.

"I liked it better before," he said.

"Before?"

"When you were in the sleeping bag with me." He pulled again on her hands. "C'mere. Please."

Darryn stood and leaned over to kiss him. He pulled her into the bed beside him.

"I think this is against the rules or something," she murmured, kissing his throat and snuggling tight to him. "Does your ankle hurt?"

"No, dammit. My pride hurts." Kirk wrapped both arms around her, despite the IV tube. "Did Yogurt tell you how it happened?"

"No, we were too worried about your temperature."

"I couldn't pay attention," Kirk said. "I kept thinking about how mean I'd acted to you because of Peter. I couldn't concentrate on the climb at all. Yogurt saw I didn't have it. He asked if I wanted to quit. But I was too stubborn to admit guilt was messing me up."

"Guilt? Over me?" Darryn nuzzled his neck. "I think I'm liking this conversation. Are you actually going to apologize?"

She expected Kirk to laugh at her teasing. He didn't even chuckle. Cradling her temples between his palms, he turned her face up to his. "A thousand times if you want. Every day for the rest of our lives."

"No, please don't." In the dim light from above his bed, Darryn could see the remorse in his gray eyes. "I'm the one who should apologize. I didn't listen to you, and you were right about—"

"No." Kirk bent to kiss her softly. "I turned out to be right about Peter, I'm sorry to say. But I shouldn't have put you in a spot like that, trapped between me and your father. I only did it because I was insanely jealous that you would go off alone with another man, share the wilderness with him, when it had meant so much to us."

"You thought that, Kirk? Why didn't you say so? I'd *never* have gone."

"I know that now. I probably knew it then." He drew in a long breath that expanded his chest against hers. "I wanted you to refuse to go with Peter on your own. I wanted you to take the first step, prove your love before I declared myself."

"That's understandable."

"The hell it is!"

"For a mulehead like you, Kirk..."

"You told me over and over that you loved me," Kirk said. "I just couldn't believe you. You seemed to want...so many things I couldn't give you without my family's money." He pulled her against him, tucking her head beneath his chin. "Do you know the first time you told me you loved me?"

Darryn didn't care at the moment. She just wanted to go on feeling Kirk's warmth and closeness, hear his heart beating, his lungs breathing, his deep wonderful alive voice. "When?"

"The night you found out about my trust fund."

"Kirk! You don't think—"

"Not anymore." He sounded remorseful. "I told myself it was just coincidence. But I kept wondering why you hadn't told me when I was a poor mountain guide."

"Oh, Kirk." Darryn pulled back to look him. "I may not have said it aloud, but I said it hundreds of times to myself. Ask Yogurt. I told him at the end of our camping trip, before I found ou—"

"I know," Kirk groaned. "Believe me, I know. Yogurt revealed that precious piece of information to me—about eight thousand times after I broke my ankle, when I couldn't get away from him." He chuckled. "I think that's why I went into shock, so I didn't have to hear him haranguing me anymore about the grave injustice I'd done you."

Kirk turned serious again. "But, Princess, I still can't give you the things you want." He stroked the hair gently past her temples. "You really are a princess, you know. And I'll never be able to treat you like one. I mean to pay my own way in this life, and with the occupation I've chosen, I'll never be rich."

"I don't want *things*, Kirk. I want you."

"You don't know what you're saying. You don't—"

"Kirk Storm," Darryn said. "You still think I'm looking for a daddy, don't you?"

Kirk stared at her, a contemplative frown creasing his brow. "It'd be pretty hard to believe that now, when *you* just rescued *me* from disaster, not the other way around."

"Do you think tonight was the first time I ever pulled my own weight?"

"I'm stubborn, not stupid. You began doing that almost as soon as I met you." He gave her a repentant grin. "It just took me awhile to admit it. Those things I said that day at your apartment... That was just jealousy talking." He kissed her eyelids. "I was so furious that you'd gone with Peter, I couldn't think straight. I was even more furious—and jealous—that he could give you things you want, and I can't. You kept mentioning money and I can't... *won't* earn enough for all those things. Darryn, I don't want four cars and a house so big I can't find my bedroom. I want only what I need."

"Kirk, I just want us to earn a little more so I can take the summers off and go with you on your trips. That's what *I* need: to be with you all the time. I couldn't bear it if you left me behind." She gripped his shoulders and shook him gently. "I'll even take your rotation at cooking. If that's not love, I don't know what it is."

Kirk's lips curved. "That's just hunger."

"I'll burn my silk suits."

His smile was fading. "That's teasing. And a waste of natural fibers."

Darryn realized Kirk was still afraid to believe her. "I learned some things this week about love, Kirk. Not just from you. I love you so much I don't think I'll ever have time to learn all about it. From my parents."

"You mean Evan?"

"Both of them." Darryn snuggled against him. "Kirk,
I like their house. I admit it. I like silk. But those things
are just comfortable. They don't make me happy. They
don't even make Mom happy. She has them *instead* of
happiness. I don't want to live that way. I've found my
happiness." She put her arms around his chest, squeezing
him tight. "I'll give up anything to keep it."

Kirk's voice came out strained. "I don't want you to
have to give up anything."

"Kirk, you thick head. Listen to me! I want *you*.
Nothing else. Giving up is what we'll do if we don't have
each other. With you, everything else is just...extra.
Without you, anything else is nothing."

"I am trying very hard to believe you." Hope glit-
tered in his gray eyes. "Even after I start the climbing
school, we won't have a lot more..." His words trailed
off.

Darryn wanted to pound on his skull. Instead she
pressed kisses to the corners of his mouth. "That's just
money, Kirk. You're my life."

Kirk's eyes looked suspiciously glisteny. "Darryn
Langtry," he said. "I don't deserve you. I don't know
why I was lucky enough to find you. But I believe you're
going to make my life worth living."

Kirk began wiggling around in the bed and Darryn
realized he was trying to get up. "Hold still. You'll hurt
your foot."

Throwing off the covers, Kirk knelt on the mattress
in front of her. "I want to do one thing, the most important thing I've ever done in my life, in the most conventional way." He lifted her hand to his lips. "Darryn,
I love you more than climbing, more than the wilderness, more than breathing. I can't live without you.
If I try, I'll probably break every bone in my body.
Will you marry me?" Leaning toward her, he kissed
her deeply.

When he raised his head, Darryn was breathing too hard to speak. She wrapped her hands behind his neck and leaned against him, toppling them both back onto the sheets. He kissed her again, sending warmth flowing through her veins.

"What a cure for hypothermia," Darryn murmured. "I wonder if it's in the first aid books."

"If you don't answer my proposal, Princess Brat, I'll..." His hands slid through the gap at the back of her nightgown. "I'll make you wear this hospital gown on all our backpacking trips."

"Answer you?" Darryn half-laughed, half-sobbed through her tears of joy. "I've been begging you to marry me for weeks, and now *you* want an answer?"

Kirk made a low growling noise and chewed on her earlobe. "Damn right, wench." He rolled on top of her, the weight of his cast pressing down on her leg. He kissed her throat till her head tipped back in delight. "Say, yes. A simple word."

"Oh yes," Darryn sighed. "As if you didn't know." She grabbed his head in her hands. "I can't believe I agreed to do all the cooking. I thought I was so liberated." She shook him. "Will you always set up the tent?"

Kirk's laugh came from deep in his chest. "A tent, a lean-to, a cabin. Anything, love, anything at all if you're going to live inside it with me." His eyes closed in an expression of intense emotion. "Darryn, don't ever go off with another man again. I couldn't take it. I didn't handle it well this time. I'd be worse next time."

Darryn's voice trembled. "As if there would ever be a next time, you dolt."

"Promise?"

"Of course I promise." She snuggled into his side. "Will you promise to give up winter climbing?"

Kirk's body froze beside her. "Darryn." He sounded anguished. "I...can't. Did you think I would?"

"Of course not," she said with a laugh, feeling tension flow out of him. "I just thought I'd ask."

"Brat," he said, giving her a swat on the backside. Then his voice turned serious. "I promise I'll never go again with fewer than four people. That'll increase the safety a hundredfold." He pressed his lips to her temple. "And I'll never go when I'm halfway through a big fight with my wife. Arguing with you seems to take my mind off climbing."

"You'll never go again without your wife, period." Darryn's voice trembled at the memory of nearly losing Kirk. "I plan to be at the foot of every climb you ever make."

Kirk lifted her head toward his and his mouth found hers.

"Ahem," said the nurse's voice from the doorway. "I don't think this is...um, a good idea."

With a whimper, Darryn pulled back from Kirk's kiss. "Oh, you're wrong. This is a wonderful idea!"

"But you have your own room down—"

Kirk's arm tightened around Darryn's shoulders. "Don't even think about it, nurse. She's staying right here." He leaned his head back against the pillows, a look of unadulterated joy lighting his face. "Forever."

Harlequin Romance®

Delightful

Affectionate

Romantic

Emotional

Tender

Original

Daring

Riveting

Enchanting

Adventurous

Moving

Harlequin Romance—the
series that has it all!

HROM-G

HARLEQUIN ◆ PRESENTS®

HARLEQUIN PRESENTS
men you won't be able to resist
falling in love with...

HARLEQUIN PRESENTS
women who have feelings
just like your own...

HARLEQUIN PRESENTS
powerful passion in
exotic international settings...

HARLEQUIN PRESENTS
intense, dramatic stories that will keep you
turning to the very last page...

HARLEQUIN PRESENTS
The world's bestselling romance series!

PRES-G